Crossing the courtyard, she opened the iron gates

Then she was away. Her bare feet made no sound as she slipped down the long, straight drive.

Dusk was rapidly turning to darkness, but Carol would not feel safe until she was on the road. Almost a half a mile away stood the two great gateposts. If only she could get to them before Nicolas realized she was gone.

After what seemed an age, the gateposts loomed large at either side, and Carol stepped out onto the road.

At last the sound of a car made her turn to face the oncoming headlights, headlights that spelled freedom and people and friends and home.

Too late, she recognized the car as Nicolas halted beside her.

"Get in," he said shortly.

Daphne Hope is a British writer living in southern England. Her background in journalism adds interest to her writing in this, her first book in the Harlequin Romance line.

Look at My Heart

Daphne Hope

Harlequin Books

TORONTO • NEW YORK • LONDON
AMSTERDAM • PARIS • SYDNEY • HAMBURG
STOCKHOLM • ATHENS • TOKYO • MILAN

Original hardcover edition published in 1987
by Mills & Boon Limited

ISBN 0-373-HRS 12

Harlequin Romance first edition April 1988

CHAPTER ONE

IF Carol had felt too lazy, or too hot, or too lacking in curiosity, to climb the steep path to the cave where Calypso was said to have lured Ulysses, this book would have ended on page one.

'The beach was golden,' it would have begun. 'The May sun tempted the three sunbathers to shut their eyes and sleep, until it was time for the last swim of their Mediterranean holiday. And on the next day, they went home.'

But Carol was more restless than lazy, more adventurous than hot, and the path called to her, pulled at her, as if it wanted her to follow and explore, promising some secret, a pleasure that was entirely its own.

Climbing the path, Carol felt herself part of the ancient hillside. The wide flat stones which paved the path were warm and grey, and worn smooth with age. From the uneven cracks between them, wild flowers, blue and yellow and crimson, burst out, covering the path with a carpet of colour so vivid, so joyful, that Carol felt exhilarated and alive.

The only sound came from the bees, nosing gently into the clover flowers, a faint rustling where the wind shook the hanging feathery grasses, and the now distant wash of waves on the beach.

She paused for breath, and turned to look down. There lay the great golden sweep of sand. With a designer's eye, Carol noticed the rocks below the deep transparent blue of the water, and stored them in one corner of her mind as a possible design for a new range of watery printed silks. She smiled as she raised one hand to wave at the sunbathers stretched out below, so far away that they looked like two figures seen through the wrong end of a telescope. Even John, her brother, big, bumbling John, looked no bigger than an Action Man doll—more of a minnow than a whale.

They lay on their fronts, toasting: Rosie slim and brown, in a golden bikini which deepened her tan, John broad and fair-haired and fit. But he'll burn, Carol judged, with critical sisterly affection. Even in May the sun was quite strong, and with the help of the sea wind was beginning to redden his back.

They had not wanted to climb the path.

'Too hot,' John had said. 'Too much like hard work.'

'And it's our last day,' Rosie had added. 'Our last chance to soak up this heavenly, heavenly sun before we have to go back. Why don't you relax? You've been working too hard at those old sketches of yours. Do you good to lie in the sun.'

But Carol had laughed and said that Rosie could relax well enough for two. She wanted to see where the path went.

'Up,' John had said. 'But if you really want to know, I can save you the trouble.' He had reached for the guidebook, looked at the index, found the page, and read:

'Ramla Bay. Not only is Ramla's sand an excellent ingredient for concrete . . .'

Rosie had snatched the book from him. 'John's hopeless. Speak to him of roses and moonlight, and he'll tell you how to make a compost heap. Yes, there it is, all tremendously romantic. "High up on the steep hill above the bay is a cave where Ulysses is reputed to have lived for seven years with the enchantress Calypso . . ."'

'A cave?' John had said. 'We saw caves yesterday, masses of them.'

'"Before the road was built,"' Rosie had read on, '"the only way up was by an ancient paved path . . ."' Oh, Carol, you'll have to go! I'd come with you, but I'm totally worn out by all that temple-trotting we did this morning.'

So Carol was alone with her path, and she was glad. It was peaceful. It was perfect.

Turning to face the hillside, Carol felt the sun warming her back as it warmed the smooth grey stone of the path, with its sprawling carpet of flowers. Taller plants grew by the side of the path: feathery fennel, purple mallow, blue borage. A brilliant thistle caught her eye, and she made a mental note of the spiky shape of the leaf, seeing the pattern it might make in a printed velvet for the winter, blue and green on grey, just as it was here, spreading in rosettes on the stone.

A small lizard ran across the path and lay in the sun, his sides heaving. Carol noticed the minute perfection of his scaly body, a tiny grey-green dragon with hooded eyes.

Wondering how much further she had to go, Carol glanced upwards. High up, to the left, screened until now by a belt of flowering trees, was a villa of yellow stone. All the buildings in Gozo were of yellow stone, which mellowed to a dusty, bleached, honey colour when they were old. When they were new, as this villa must be, the stone was bright, like gold.

Silhouetted against the golden wall of the villa was a man, looking down, frowning.

Never before had Carol been so aware of another person. It was almost like touching an electric fence. The shock was physical, making her heart jump, leaving her breathless.

The man was tall—toweringly tall, Carol thought at first, but perhaps that was because he was looking down at her, and she up at him. He was dark, his skin so deeply tanned that he must, surely, be a resident rather than a visitor, and his hair was black, but smooth, with none of the exuberant curl of the Maltese fishermen. His mouth was set in a line which would have been grim, even cruel, if the creases round it had not shown that it was a mouth which could smile.

But it was the eyes which held her. Looking directly down into hers, they had the same dark intensity as the sea behind her. He was a cool one, Carol thought, to stare at her so unwaveringly, and with such a formidable glare. As a girl with more than her fair share of good looks, she was used to people noticing her, but generally they looked away when she stared back. And this, she realised, was exactly what she was doing. She blinked, and glanced down at the path. The lizard which had been sunning itself ran into a crack between two blocks of stone and disappeared. When she looked up again, the man was gone.

Carol felt a small pang of disappointment. She had to admit that she had looked up with a feeling of excitement. Then she shrugged her shoulders. Probably only a tourist, after all, she thought, frowning into the sun, not at her. No—he had most certainly been looking at her. Carol remembered the acute awareness she had felt when she found herself the object of that fierce, dark stare.

As the path brought her level with the pillared wall of the new villa, she looked curiously at the statues which guarded the four corners of a wide terrace, at the fountain which did not, as yet, play water into a shallow basin. The villa was not finished. A load of yellow stone blocks lay in a haphazard heap at one side of the terrace, with builders' tools flung down beside them.

So that was the answer. The man was a workman, possibly one who did not like being interrupted by casual passers-by. Compared with the easy-natured Maltese, the

Gozitan was—not surly—more reserved and proud, and independent. Still, Carol wished she had asked him where she would find Calypso's cave. Either she had somehow missed the place, or the guidebook was very out of date. A little track led off on one side to a few depressions in the ground, some grey boulders and a flattened space where someone had dropped a crumpled cigarette packet. There was no sign of a cave, and Carol went back to the original path.

This very soon came to an end, meeting the main road where it swung round a corner and up the hill. On the right, perched above the path, was a small yellow square house with a notice in the window, saying 'Postcards and Gozo Lace'.

So lace still was made in Gozo—she must tell Rosie. Rosie had put forward a theory that lace had been replaced by knitting as the national craft, though John had insisted that lace-making was traditional, and quoted the guidebook to prove it. Rosie had laughed, and said she would have to see it to believe it.

And now here it was. Carol would have to go in. She had some money in the pocket of her blue cotton skirt. Perhaps there would be a handkerchief or something small she could buy, to show Rosie that the guidebook was right, after all.

As she made her way round the corner of the house, Carol saw an old woman, all in black, sitting outside her open door, making lace, as if she were a living illustration for the notice in the window. She sat on a wooden chair and had a long, narrow, sausage-shaped pillow propped on the back of another chair in front of her. The pillow was hung with bobbins, clustering from a web of fine white cotton. The fingers which held the flying bobbins were gnarled and bent, but the web they were making was as delicate as a cobweb.

The old woman looked up at Carol with a smile of great serenity. She had wide-set eyes, kind and untroubled, and deep slanting lines from her nose to the corners of her mouth. Her hair was pulled back, with no parting, into a bun and, despite her age, was jet black, with no hint of grey in it. No spectacles, Carol noticed—and such fine work.

'*Merhba.*' The lace-maker gave Carol the greeting which she had come to know. 'You wish to see my lace? Come inside. I have much lace, and it is beautiful. Come, and I show you.'

The room was cool and shaded, dark after the sunshine outside. Two tables against one wall were covered with samples of her work: neat piles of mats and napkins, and handkerchiefs folded to show the corners with their designs of flowers and leaves and little birds. On another wall was pinned a magnificent tablecloth.

'How beautiful!' said Carol, and the old woman smiled.

'That one,' she said, pointing to the lace cloth on the wall, 'that was two years to make. So it is very much money. One hundred pounds, too much for people to buy.'

A hundred pounds for two years' work seemed modest enough, Carol thought. No wonder the younger women had taken to knitting.

'But wait,' said the old lace-maker, 'I have something even more beautiful to show you,' and she disappeared through a bead curtain into a back room, coming out after a moment with a flat cardboard dress box which she put carefully on the table.

Carol wondered what could be inside to be treated with such care—a priest's robe, perhaps? An altar cloth? It must be something very special to be swathed in so many layers of tissue paper. At last came the gleam of silk, and the old woman pulled out fold after fold of what seemed to be another fine lace cloth. Then Carol saw it was a wedding veil.

She caught her breath. It was lovely, as fine as gossamer, but with the rich, creamy colour of pearls. The old woman held it up.

'Try it,' she said. Lovingly, almost compellingly, she draped the veil over Carol's fair hair, pinning it into place, and turned her to face a looking-glass which hung on the wall.

It was an old glass, with worn silvering, so that the background was a pool of shadow out of which the veil floated and shone. Carol had little time to gaze at her own reflection. There was a sound of footsteps, as someone threw the door open behind her, and a harsh exclamation, making an explosion of sound in the quiet room.

In the depths of the mirror, behind her own image, stood the man Carol had seen on the hillside, the man who had stared at her from the wall of the unfinished villa. The suddenness of his appearance made her jump; it was as if he were an apparition from some darker region of the world. There was something in his face which made Carol afraid, for an instant. Besides anger there was passion. Then it was gone, and only the anger remained.

'So!' he said. 'This is how you amuse yourself!' And before Carol could say a word, he grasped her wrist in a grip which hurt, and swung her round to face him.

'Let me go!' Carol said, in shocked amazement.

The old woman looked from one to the other in bewilderment, and then melted into the darkness of the other room.

At the sound of Carol's voice, the man dropped her wrist and stood back, looking at her, all his anger gone. In its place was an expression of sardonic amusement.

'It seems that I must ask you to forgive me,' he said, with

the air of a man who did not think forgiveness really necessary.

Carol lifted her chin. He was so tall that she had to look up to meet his gaze, which annoyed her.

'Will you explain?' she said. 'Or am I talking to a madman?'

She wished she was taller. She felt at a ridiculous disadvantage, talking to somebody with her head and shoulders draped in a bridal veil, and tugged at the pins which fastened it to her hair.

'No,' he said. 'Leave it,' and his voice had such a ring of authority that Carol, in spite of herself, obeyed. 'Enough time has been wasted already. I can assure you that I am not mad—you can ask Ta Dentella, if you must—and I will explain everything in the car, as we go along.'

'Indeed you will not,' said Carol. 'Storming in here— then physical assault——' She rubbed her wrist where she could still feel the pressure from his fingers. 'The barest of apologies—and then you think I will do whatever you ask! Do you tell everyone what to do? And do they always do it?'

'Generally,' he said, frowning a little with impatience. 'When they understand that it is the best thing for them to do.'

'And how do you convince them?' said Carol, feeling her courage return. 'Is it with persuasive argument, or sheer charm of manner?'

If she had expected the frowning stranger to be at all put out by her sarcasm, she was disappointed. A gleam of humour came into his eyes, and his mouth, which had been set in a grim straight line, relaxed into something approaching a smile.

'If you want charm,' he said, 'you will have to wait. For the moment . . .' In a single quick movement he strode forward and picked up Carol as if she were a child. 'You are small and I am large. I am in all probability a good deal stronger than you. Add to that the fact that I have a reputation for ruthlessness, especially if it is a matter of getting my own way, and that I am a man, and you are . . .' He paused, while he set her on her feet outside the little house, beside the low red sports car which stood waiting. 'A woman. I hope you will not force me to throw you into the car. Will you get in?' He opened the door on the passenger side, and held it, waiting.

'You could say "please",' said Carol, flustered and angry, but determined not to show fear before this impulsive lunatic.

At first his frown returned. Then he gave her a smile of such genuine warmth and friendliness that Carol, at that moment, stopped being afraid.

'Please,' he said, the smile broadening, his eyes holding hers in what she felt was an exercise of will-power. 'As a favour—a great favour to me. It will save time if you will just get in,' he said, impatience edging his voice as she still hesitated.

Carol laughed. 'On the understanding that I am doing you a favour, then,' she said, 'and that you will bring me back in—half an hour? My brother is down there, on the beach, and he'll be ringing the police if I just disappear. Couldn't I at least leave him a note to say where I am?'

'No time,' said the stranger, 'and no need. Ta Dentella will reassure him, if he should take it into his head to pursue you.' The old woman was looking out at them both, from a window. She smiled, and raised her hand, as if in a blessing. 'You see? She will be able to tell him that you are in safe hands. And we shall probably be back in half an hour. I am in as great a hurry as you.'

That he was in a hurry was all too clear, Carol thought,

by the speed with which he drove. As he sent the car screeching in the yellow dust round the first corner, Carol wonderd that she felt no alarm, only a sense of elation and adventure.

'And in whose safe hands am I?' she asked. They whirled past two men cutting blocks of yellow stone by the side of the road, a gaggle of schoolchildren, and an old man with a donkey cart loaded as high as a house with grass.

'My name is Nicolas,' said the man by her side. 'Xatahn.' He pronounced it with the X making a sound between 'sh' and a soft 'j'. 'My family calls me Nick, and my friends——' his teeth gleamed in a sudden smile '——Satan, I believe, but not to me. And you?'

Carol told him her name, thinking how well the name of Satan fitted his dark looks. They had come to one of the little towns which in Gozo are no bigger than villages, and sped past a group of black-haired women knitting under a tree in the small square. They looked up from their work, but the car had left them behind before Carol had a chance to see if they were in any way surprised to see her in the passenger seat. She must be an odd sight, trying to control the flying ends of the delicate lace veil.

She was so occupied in holding on to these with one hand, and to the side of the car with the other, in order to avoid being flung against Nicolas as he tore round the bends of the road, that she was barely able to take in what he was telling her.

It was something about the film company which was making a historical film on the island—there had been talk about it in the hotel, Carol remembered—and a missing star, the leading lady, who had been threatening to pack her bags and leave, and could not now be found.

By the scorn in his voice as he spoke of the film people, Carol guessed that Nicolas did not approve of them, and would be glad when they went.

'So without a leading lady, they cannot finish the film,' he ended.

'Then you should be pleased,' Carol said.

'But I want them to finish it, and go!' he said. 'They are paying me well for the privilege of using my land, but if they wait for the temperamental Madrilena to come back, they will be bankrupt. And now the leading man has also said that he will leave if she is not found. I hope we shall not arrive too late.'

'We shan't arrive anywhere if you drive like this,' Carol felt like saying. She would not have hesitated to say it to her brother, but judged it wiser to leave the words unsaid with a driver as headstrong as Nicolas. They were driving now along a narrow road so near the edge of a steep cliff that Carol did not dare to look towards the seaward side.

'What I don't see,' she said, valiantly overcoming a desire to shut her eyes and clutch at his arm, 'is where I come into all this. *I* haven't seen your missing actress. I don't even know what she looks like.'

'That, my dear girl,' said Nicolas, driving apparently straight at the cliff edge, and turning only at the last moment as the road snaked down in a series of sharp hairpin bends, 'that is precisely the point.'

A small crowd of people—cameramen, actors in costume, a girl with a notebook, a man with a megaphone—appeared in front of them and, with a protesting scream of brakes, the red car came to a stop.

The effect its arrival had on the crowd was as dramatic as if someone had waved a magic wand. Every face turned towards them; every figure stayed perfectly still, for the space of a second, in a tableau of surprise.

Then the man with the megaphone sprang forward to meet them. He wore sunglasses, a white linen hat, an orange and red T-shirt and blue shorts. He was a small man, but a pointed beard gave his face an air of importance, and he radiated energy in every direction.

'*Mon cher* Baron! You have found her?' he said. 'But it's not possible. We had a *coup de téléphone* from Sicily. How could she be there and here at the same time? The telephone call was another of her *diableries*, perhaps?'

He turned to Carol. 'Look at these! Do you know how much they are costing me a minute?' With a sweep of his arm he embraced the crowd of sailors, peasants and cameramen. 'Why do you play this game of cat and mouse with me? How can you blow hot and cold? Some things you do like an angel, and then—*diable!*—we have another tantrum. You do not like the wedding gown: it is too tight, you cannot breathe! You must leave at once! You cannot tolerate your leading man! I—Varelle—am a monster! I do not treat you with respect. You refuse to do the wedding scenes! And what is that you have round your head if it is not a wedding veil?'

During the whole of this tirade, which made Carol wonder if she had been brought by one madman to be confronted with another, Nicolas sat silent, his arms folded, smiling in a peculiarly infuriating way.

'Tell him,' said Carol at last, when the little man drew breath, 'tell him that I haven't the faintest idea what he's talking about. And will you please tell me why you have brought me here to be raved at?'

Nicolas raised his eyebrows. 'I should have thought that was perfectly clear,' he said.

'Perfectly,' said Carol. She made a determined effort to pull out the hairpins which had kept the veil in place, and at last succeeded. 'First you abduct me. Then you drive as though you wanted to kill us both. And now——' she threw the veil back and away from her hair until it rested on her

shoulders '—now you seem to be trying to pass me off as
somebody else!'

The man with the beard stared at her. He had been about
to begin another monologue, she saw, but now it was like
seeing a film with the sound switched off. His lips moved,
but no sound came from them.

Then he came over to Nicolas and clapped him on the
shoulder, bursting into a roar of laughter.

'You are a miracle worker, my friend. A sorcerer—no, a
conjurer. How do you find her? Don't tell me. I know. All
you had to do was to stand by some magic pool in your
enchanted island, and mutter some incantation, *et voilà*, we
have an actress once more!'

Carol started. 'I'm not an actress,' she said. 'I've never
acted in my life.'

Nicolas smiled. 'It was almost like that,' he said to
Varelle. 'I found her in a very suitable place, near Calypso's
cave. I was as deceived as you were. I quite thought I had
found *la belle* Madrilena. At first, when I saw her on the
path, I was not sure, but when I found her in Ta Dentella's
house, and wearing a wedding veil, I—like you—thought
that she was playing one of her tricks.'

So that was why he had gazed down at her so intently
from the villa, Carol thought. Not because she attracted
him in any way; it was because she had looked like someone
else.

'I understand now why you behaved like a maniac, back
there,' she said. 'But I still don't see why you brought me
here. You said I could help you, but I can't. And if you
think I can take the place of an actress in a film, you must be
even more crazy than I thought you were to begin with. I
can't act. My voice is quite different—you said so yourself.
And I'm going home tomorrow. There's no possible way in
which I can help you.'

Both men looked at her, Nicolas with a smile of appreciation in his eyes, the other appraisingly, his head on one side.

'But who is she?' said the bearded man. 'I have never seen her among the extras. I would have remembered. That hair—it will have to be dyed. Or a wig.' He turned and shouted. 'Kate, Kate! A dark wig. *Vite, vite*! Straight, of course, like Madrilena. Hurry! And tell Antonio all is well.' He turned back to Nicolas, who was unfolding himself from the car. 'Nick, my friend, her name?'

'You promised to take me back,' Carol said, as imperiously as she could. 'My brother will be sending out search parties for me.' But when Nicolas held out his hand to help her out, she found herself taking it.

'First, you must allow me to introduce Monsieur Georges Varelle,' he said. 'He is a director, and will be the first to tell you how popular his films are. Monsieur Varelle, Miss Goodwin. Her name is Carol, though I myself prefer Calypso.'

'Monsieur Varelle,' Carol said, disregarding Nicolas, 'I am sorry, but I really can't help you. It's out of the question . . .'

She might have been a bird twittering for all the impact her words made. Varelle studied her, cocking his head first on one side, then on the other.

'Good figure,' he said, 'and about the same size. Nothing to worry about in the long shots. Most of the wedding ceremony is from the back. We can cut the close-ups to a minimum. The whole wedding feast is complete already. Yes, my friend, she might do. She might indeed.'

Carol appealed to Nicolas. 'Tell him,' she said. 'Tell him that whatever it is he wants me to do, *I will not do it*!'

She raised her voice, and this time Varelle seemed to have heard her, for he looked up in astonishment.

'My dear Nick, your protégée is angry. Why is this? Don't tell me that you have brought her here without explaining.' He shook his head, and addressed Carol for the first time.

'Miss Goodwin, what must you think of me? That I am as terrible a monster as Nick here? For that I shall not forgive him. Come, you must sit down.' He clapped his hands and shouted, 'Chairs! You are hot, and thirsty, I expect. Drinks! And ice! Here, sit. For just five minutes, no more, I promise you.' And, as Carol began again to protest, 'At least you will permit me to give you some fresh lemon.'

It was just like being on a stage set. One man brought three folding chairs, another a tray with tall glasses. Varelle gave her one glass, and Nicolas another, and sat back in his chair.

'There, that is better. Now we can be comfortable. You know something of our difficulties?'

'Only that you have lost your leading lady. You can't be serious if you imagine I can take her place.'

'Wait, my dear child. If you will hear me out, you will soon see that it is not so impossible, and that all our little problems may be quickly solved. My budget will be saved, and the film finished. Nick here will be glad to see the last of us. Oh, yes, this is so, my friend. And all due to you, *mademoiselle*. Such luck! It is providence.'

Carol tasted her drink, which was sharp and ice-cold. 'I don't see . . .'

'Wait, wait, and I will tell you. There is so very little of the film to make now, that almost it does not matter that we have lost our principal actress. But that little is of vital importance.'

Rapidly he sketched for Carol the outline of the scenes which were left. A wedding procession from the harbour to the chapel. Then the wedding itself . . .

'But if her face is veiled,' Carol said, 'anyone could do it. You don't need a look-alike.'

'You are wrong,' said Varelle. 'At the end of the ceremony, the bride throws back her veil, and shows her face for the first time to the bridegroom. He is one of the Corsairs—it is a forced wedding, you understand—and he is astonished to see that he has abducted his own sweetheart. He sees her face, *et voilà*! It is the girl he has loved from many years before, and never thought to see again. He *must* see her face, and the audience must see also.' He leaned forward and gazed imploringly at Carol. 'Just one little scene—it is all I ask.'

'I see,' said Carol. 'And you think I would do?'

'Do! You would be perfect. An answer to prayer. Say that you will. Just one, at most two little scenes.'

He kept his hypnotic gaze on Carol, as if the fate of thousands hung on her answer.

'You asked for the wig, Monsieur Varelle.' A girl appeared behind his chair. Varelle leapt to his feet. 'Good! Now, at once, we will try . . .' And before Carol could say anything, the girl was fitting it to Carol's head with expert fingers, smoothing her fair hair out of sight.

'Perfect,' said Varelle. 'Nick, do you not think so? Come, for the moment you can take the part of the Corsair. Where is Antonio? He must be told. Now, the veil. It must be arranged.'

'I will arrange it,' said Nicolas, unexpectedly. He picked it up from Carol's shoulders and placed it gently over her hair so that it fell, half hiding her face. Through the folds of the veil, Carol saw that he was looking intently at her. Again she felt the same shock of excitement she had experienced when she first saw him on the hillside.

Of course she couldn't stay, to act in a film. The idea was ridiculous. She had to go back to England with Rosie and

John. Or had she? Her partner would be expecting her, waiting for the sketches for Célie et Cie. If she did stay, John would take them for her. He was as reliable as the Bank of England.

Varelle was shifting round Nicolas and Carol, making exclamations of delight. 'Perfect!' he said. 'Better than I could have imagined. Take her hand, my dear Nick.'

Nicolas took her hand and held it in a grip which made Carol catch her breath.

'And you, *mademoiselle*, throw back the veil, and look into his eyes.'

Carol did as she was told, and felt his hand tighten on hers. She hoped that he could not guess at the idiotic leap of her heart as she met the look from those intensely dark eyes.

Nicolas smiled into her face. 'You will do it?' he asked her.

'As a favour to you?' she said.

'As a great favour to me,' he repeated.

It was only later, when Varelle had kissed her hand, and Nicolas had driven her back to Ramla, and driven away again to return the veil to its owner, that Carol realised why she had agreed to such an extraordinary scheme. If she were honest with herself, she had to admit that it all had to do with the dark looks and compelling personality of Nicolas, Baron Xatahn.

'What's he like, your Baron?' Rosie asked, when Carol told them of the change in her plans. 'Is he old and fat, or young and devastatingly handsome? Or wicked, like a panto-mime baron?'

'He's . . .' Carol hesitated. What was the most outstand-ing thing about Nicolas? His height? His disconcerting way of looking at people? His commanding manner? Or the way he assumed that everyone would do what he wanted, even Varelle?

'He's the kind of man who likes to get his own way,' she said.

'Wouldn't suit you, then,' said her brother. 'How did he manage to drag you into this mad scheme of his?'

'It's not really his scheme,' Carol said, 'and it isn't *so* mad. If you both stayed on another two days, I could come back with you as we'd planned. Couldn't you?'

'Not a hope,' said John. 'I've a meeting fixed for Monday, and anyway our flights are booked.'

Unbook them, Carol suddenly felt like saying. Unbook them, and stay with me. But she knew that it would be like talking to the Rock of Gibraltar and, in any case, what was there to fear?

CHAPTER TWO

CAROL stood on the quayside at Mgarr, waving goodbye to John and Rosie. In the harbour the small and brightly painted fishing boats bobbed and curtsied to the wind, and the ferry, *Queen of Gozo*, had already passed the long arm of the breakwater. Her pale blue hull was shining in the early sun, and on deck John and Rosie were still waving.

Carol felt a surge of affection for them both: Rosie with her sense of fun, John so safe and square and sensible. She could trust him, she knew, to deliver her precious designs safely to the studio.

'I hope you know what you're doing,' he had said at dinner, the evening before.

'Of course she does,' Rosie had insisted. 'She's going to be the most tremendous success—and the next time we see her we'll probably have to fight our way through a police cordon for her autograph. If the wicked Baron hasn't spirited her away to his castle keep, of course!'

'The next time you see me will be next week,' Carol had said. Rosie's last remark she had ignored. But now, standing and gazing at the ever smaller and more distant ferry, she did wonder fleetingly if she would see anything of Nicolas, Baron of Xatahn, during the coming day.

'Hello there—Carol?' A voice startled her, and she looked round; she had not heard the Land Rover drive up behind her. A girl leaned out of the driver's window and smiled. 'Varelle sent us to fetch you,' she said. 'We tried the hotel, and they told us you'd be here.'

23

For the space of a heartbeat, Carol took the dark man sitting beside the girl to be Nicolas. But a second glance showed her that this man was paler and thinner than the Baron. Although he was good-looking enough, there was a blankness of expression which had nothing in common with Nicolas's fierce and penetrating stare.

'Meet Tony,' said the girl with the friendly smile. 'Your leading man. And I'm Kate. Costumes, props, bottlewasher, girl Friday, etcetera.'

'I couldn't wait to inspect my new leading lady,' said Tony, smiling also. 'The other one was a hell-cat. Are you a hell-cat? No, I can see you're not. Quite the opposite. I'm sure we shall get along most beautifully.'

Carol was fascinated, and amused to see that he was putting on a performance for her. All the way up the winding road from the harbour, past the Uptodate Garage and the Gleneagles Bar, he was being the Great Actor for her benefit.

'What's on the menu for today, sweetheart?' he asked Kate. 'She knows everything, but everything,' he told Carol. 'It's her job, of course, but she's terribly good at it.'

'Turkish fleet comes in—only two ships actually—this morning. Wedding procession meets the fleeing masses in the afternoon. Citadel goes up in flames this evening,' said Kate in a matter-of-fact way. 'Though where he'll get the extras for his fleeing masses when everyone's at the carnival is anyone's guess.'

'What does the great man say about it?' Tony asked.

'Won't listen, as usual,' said Kate. 'You know what he's like if something happens to upset the master plan. Doesn't want to hear.'

'It all sounds very dramatic,' said Carol.

'Hasn't anyone told you the story of the film?' said Tony.

'My dearest one, it's highly dramatic, romantic, and all the other 'icks' you can think of—bombastic, idiotic, and just plain . . .'

'Tony, shut up,' said Kate. 'You know you enjoy being a bold Corsair. He's the Corsair captain,' she told Carol, as they turned off the main road into a narrow side lane. 'The Turks were always raiding Gozo, you see, and in 1551 they came in a fleet of a hundred and forty galleys.'

'Chap called Sinam Baxa,' put in Tony.

'He besieged the citadel. Everyone on the island was hiding inside for refuge,' Kate went on. 'And when he'd taken it, he carried off six thousand slaves—that was all the Gozitans, except for the few who managed to escape.'

'Let down by ropes over the ramparts by night,' said Tony. 'You've seen those ramparts? Terrifying!'

'How does the Corsair captain come into it?' Carol asked. 'I mean, why a marriage, if he's a Turk?'

'Ah, but he wasn't really a Turk,' said Kate. 'He was a Gozitan, a fisherman, captured when he was eighteen by a gang of raiders.' The Land Rover was bumping over a stony track lined with tall grey-green hedges of prickly pear. 'He'd put out to sea in despair because he couldn't marry the girl he loved.'

'Family the most high-born in the island,' said Tony. 'Said he wasn't good enough.'

'When the Turks seized him, he proved such a good sailor that they promoted him, and went on promoting him till he commanded his own ship.'

'But then, along comes the Great Invasion, and the poor chap's ordered to head the fleet against his own people. Frightful dilemma.'

'Don't forget that he *is* embittered against them,

especially the girl's family. You're terribly embittered, aren't you, Tony?'

'Anyone would be embittered if they had to act with Madrilena,' said Tony.

'Hush,' said Kate. 'She could be quite good when she wasn't throwing a temperament. She did the high-born bit like a dream. Here we are, back at the ranch. Hello, what's up?'

A small boy of about five stood bawling by the side of the road. Kate stopped the Land Rover, and Carol jumped out.

'Whatever's the matter?' she asked, and put her arms round the child to console him. 'Are you hurt?'

Shaken by sobs, the boy could not speak, but then, through his tears, he gasped, 'My rabbit! My Pietro! My rabbit . . .'

A magnified roar of rage made them all jump. Fifty yards away Varelle was standing on a camera van, with a loudhailer to his mouth.

'Stand away!' he shouted. 'Imbeciles! Saboteurs! Kate, what are you doing to me?'

'The cameras!' said Carol. 'They're shooting a scene. But . . .' she looked down at the sobbing child, '. . . he's not acting.'

'Better leave him alone,' said Tony from the car, 'or you'll have Varelle exploding in small pieces.'

'Oh, blow Varelle!' said Kate. 'He's gone too far. I wouldn't put it past him to let Pietro out. Has Pietro escaped?' she asked the child.

The boy nodded, and burst into fresh tears.

'Don't cry,' said Kate. 'I'm sure we'll find him again. Didn't you put the catch on?'

'I did. I did!' said the child passionately. 'Someone let him out.'

'It's his pet rabbit,' Kate explained to Carol. 'He always brings him—puts his hutch in the shade, picks clover for him. It's a shame . . .'

'Kate! Carol! What are you doing?' Varelle had arrived at a run and was shaking with rage. 'At last—at last I have a shot of a child desolate at the loss of his mother, his father, his whole family . . .' His voice trembled with suppressed fury. '. . . and what do you do but ruin it!'

'If you look behind you,' Tony said drily, 'you'll see his real mother. She looks just a tiny bit cross.'

Sure enough, a Gozitan woman dressed as a sixteenth-century villager was hurrying towards them.

'You'd better let me deal with this,' Kate said, and as she spoke soothingly to the woman and the little boy, Varelle hurried Carol away from the scene, holding her by the elbow and talking all the time. His anger had dropped from him like a flung-off coat.

'My dear child, you are lovelier even than I thought yesterday. It is a miracle that our good Baron should find you. Elaine! Elaine!' He clapped his hands, and the girl who had brought the wig to him the day before emerged from the door of one of the caravans and ran towards them.

Everyone ran, it seemed, when Varelle clapped his hands.

'This is Elaine,' he told Carol. 'She also performs miracles. She will make you up until not even Madrilena herself could tell the difference between you. Now go, go—all of you. Carlos, you look like a priest, but do you think like a priest? Where is Antonio? Why is Kate not here?' He dashed away, shouting orders, countermanding them, leaving little whirlpools of crisis in his wake.

'Dervish,' said Elaine shortly, leading the way back to her caravan. 'If he isn't dancing about, he's behaving like

Napoleon. You may not have noticed it yet, but we rather go in for power complexes here, what with him *and* the very noble Baron.' Her voice was sharp and cutting, not quite a sneer.

'Is the Baron often here?' Carol asked.

Elaine flung back her smooth curtain of fair hair and glanced sideways at Carol. Her eyes were like a Siamese cat's, Carol thought: narrowed, appraising.

'Often enough,' she said, as she settled Carol into a chair in front of the wide mirror. 'And that reminds me—has no one given you a warning in that direction?'

'What do you mean?' Carol asked, meeting the other girl's unfriendly eyes in the mirror.

'He's a famous hunter,' said Elaine, and began to smooth cream into Carol's face with fingers which dug painfully into the skin. 'Not game. Not like the village boys taking pot shots at the pigeons.'

'What, then?' Carol asked.

'Women,' Elaine said. 'They hunt pigeons; he hunts women. It's quite cold-blooded,' she added, watching Carol's face. 'A matter of pride. He can't see a good-looking girl without adding her to his game list. I hate to tell you this, of course, but you really ought to know.'

'Oh?' said Carol. She felt uncomfortable under the other's scrutiny. 'What makes you think the Baron of Xatahn might be interested in me?'

'Oh, I don't know.' Elaine looked away. 'A new face—a new challenge. And the way he was looking at you yesterday, when I brought the wig.'

Carol's heart started its involuntary keep-fit exercises. 'How was he looking at me?' The words were out before she could stop them. She wished she could unsay them. There was a look of sly triumph on Elaine's face as she answered.

'Of course,' she said. 'I've never actually seen an eagle marking down a foolish little dove for its prey, but that's the sort of look I mean.'

'Thanks for the compliment,' said Carol. And why bother to warn me? she would have added, but from outside there came a sudden roar of rage, and Kate put her head round the door to say,

'Quick! Haven't you finished? Varelle's out for blood. He's been giving the cameramen hell over the long shots of the ships all morning. Why any of us works for him when we could do something peaceful, like road-mending, or lion-taming, I don't know.'

'What's the fuss now?' Elaine asked, binding Carol's hair back with a tight band of tape. 'Who's he bawling out this time?'

'Carlos. Varelle caught him in a poker game. "If you are to play a priest," he said, "you behave like a priest. Go and say some prayers!" And he swept the cards off the table. Carlos is hopping mad. For once he had a winning hand. Anyway, can you speed things up? Do the wig, and then hustle her round to me, and we'll do a quick change act in the wardrobe van.'

Standing among the rows of shining silk and brocade costumes, Carol admired the deftness with which Kate laced up the straight, constricting corset, and fastened the wide petticoats round her waist. They were of pale apricot silk to match the underbodice with its full loose sleeves. The russet-coloured brocade overdress with its bell-shaped skirt was so stiff that it could almost stand by itself. The high wings of the collar framed Carol's face with an under-edging of lace, and the heavy sleeves were slashed to show the pale silk beneath.

'Not too tight?' said Kate. 'Madrilena practically refused

to wear it. Said she couldn't breathe in it, let alone act. That's what the fuss was about—some of it.'

'She had a point,' said Carol. 'It makes me feel like a richly dressed doll.'

'Shoes!' said Kate. 'I've been praying you're a five.' The slippers were tight. They were of apricot brocade with orange-red heels.

'Good,' said Kate. 'Now the embroidered gloves. I'll fix the veil later or you won't see where you're going. Nervous?'

'Quite,' said Carol.

'No need,' Kate reassured her. 'You look terrific. Just pretend you're a walking doll. Great! Let's hope his Excellency is pleased.'

Varelle, when they found him outside, looked about as pleased as Jove getting ready to hurl thunderbolts about. He stood on the cliff top looking down the steep zig-zag road to the anchorage of the pirate fleet, and, as Carol and Kate approached, he flung out an arm in a gesture of impatience. Keeping his voice under control by an obvious effort, he said '*Mgarr Ix-Xini*—Harbour for Galleys. And the headland—*Ras in Newwiela*. Do you know what that means? It means "The place where the prisoners embark!" The six thousand wretches who are to be sold into slavery.' His voice rose, in a dramatic crescendo. 'Six thousand!'

Carol took her cue from Kate, who was gazing out to sea, saying nothing.

'You see that road,' Varelle went on, dropping his voice to a whisper. 'Regard it, winding down. Now shut your eyes. Imagine six thousand people, young men, women, children, being driven like goats down that rocky path to the ships that are to take them away for ever. Six thousand people! Do you see them? No, keep your eyes shut. It is like a river of people, A flood of terrified, defeated peasants, noblemen, farmers. Can you see it?'

'Yes,' said Carol. She could almost hear the shouts of the invaders, herding their human booty to the sea.

'Now open your yes,' he commanded. 'What do you see?' 'Nothing?'

'Precisely,' said Varelle. 'Nothing. Not one peasant. No shrieking women. No wailing children. Not even a goat do I see. I do not ask six thousand. That I know is outside my budget. But a great deal may be arranged with a mere three hundred. And where are they?'

He turned on his heel, and saw Tony coming towards them.

'Antonio! My brave pirate captain. I am a deranged man, a man persecuted by fate. I have my leading actor. I have my leading lady. I have my sailors—only a few, but some. The light is perfect, the colours unrivalled.' He paused. No one dared to speak. 'And now, I ask you, where are my crowds? Where are my multitudes? Where is my river of humanity?'

Tony, unruffled, smoothed the fingers of one jewelled glove.

'My dear Director,' he said. 'Ask Nicolas, not me. You engaged your crowds through him. It's his land. His—if I may say so—pigeon.'

'The Baron! Of course,' said Varelle, whirling round to Kate. 'Send for him.'

'Send for Nicolas? Are you serious?' said Kate.

'Then I shall telephone.' And Varelle raced away, followed by Kate.

'And what do you think of our wicked Baron?' Tony said lightly to Carol.

'Wicked?' said Carol. 'Is he?'

'With those eyebrows, and that black-as-night hair, he must be,' said Tony. 'Nobody could look so like a demon king without being simply steeped in wickedness. Besides, rumour has it that he has had at least three brides-to-be.'

'Rumour isn't noted for telling the truth,' Carol said, feeling that she should defend the absent Nicolas. 'And only brides-to-be? What happened to them?'

'History doesn't relate,' said Tony.

'So there's no Baroness?'

'Only his mother. Very *grande dame*. Keeps everyone up to the mark—except Big Bad Nicolas, of course.'

'You don't like him, do you?' said Carol.

'It's mutual. Nothing he does or says. Just the scornful way he looks at one, as if actors aren't quite real.'

'Perhaps he's right,' Carol was about to say, but was stopped by the return of Varelle, his face now beaming.

'It is the carnival! Why did Kate not remind me? It is her job to prevent me making these *bêtises*. Apparently,' he went on, 'the second weekend in May is always *en fête*, for Gozo as well as for Malta. All day there are processions, and at night fireworks. Half the island puts on fancy dress or beats a drum or dances in the street. The other half assembles to watch.'

'So there'll be no crowd scenes today?' said Tony. 'Couldn't we do the wedding procession up from the harbour?'

'No. No. No!' Varelle shouted. 'You do not have my vision, or you would not suggest so crazy a thing. I must have the wedding party, very far away, very small, at the bottom of the defile—a detail in the corner of my broad canvas. Then, rushing down towards it, my wide river of slaves. The people spilling down, so fast, so close together, so ravaged with despair. No, no, my dear Antonio, I shall not split this vision.'

'What, then?' said Tony.

'Nicolas has suggested that we go to lunch with him. All of us. In his *palazzo*.'

'Lucky old us,' said Tony, but Kate told him not to be so sarcastic; it was an honour; and she, for one, had been longing to see inside. 'I expect it's very grand,' she told Carol. 'A real palace.'

Carol did not know quite what kind of a place she had expected Nicolas to live in: a grim, stark fortress perhaps, perched on a rocky headland, or a Gothic pile, all towers and pinnacles. In fact it was neither.

They drove first through the rocky, flower-filled countryside, and then along a road between stone walls crowned with grey prickly pear, until they came to two great gateposts, with a coat of arms just visible in the ancient crumbling stone. They turned in through these, and down a narrow private drive with rosemary growing from tumbledown walls. The *palazzo*, when at last they came to it, was a revelation.

Far from being stark or grim, its faded pink walls were curtained with climbing plants. Flowering trees shaded the entrance, where a rounded archway, with delicately wrought iron gates thrown back, led them through to a courtyard.

At the top of a flight of worn stone steps, Nicolas stood, looking down, surveying them.

His gaze embraced all the company, but as it rested on her, for no more than the fraction of a second, Carol hoped that no one could see the colour rush to her face, or hear the pounding thump of her heart.

She felt again the tension between them, taut as steel,

electric as lightning, that she had known when Nicolas had first looked down at her, that other time, on the path. It was disturbing. Carol had never before met a man who had such a sudden and devastating effect on her. She was not sure if she liked it. Up to now, her feelings had always been under her own control. It was not altogether pleasant to find that she was no longer mistress of her emotions.

'Welcome to Xatahn,' Nicolas said. He led them through the rooms so briskly that Carol gained no more than a swift impression of slow-moving fans in high ceilings, of gilt-framed portraits on the walls, brilliant cloths thrown over chairs, polished tables, great bowls of flowers, marble floors, and wide french windows which opened on to a broad terrace, dappled with shade.

Here the luncheon was laid on a long table almost the length of the terrace. Crystal glasses, a white linen cloth, glittering silver, and more flowers in shallow bowls all gave the appearance of a banquet. As soon as Nicolas had seated them all, two servants appeared, silently and unobtrusively, and filled the glasses with wine.

'There is water if you prefer,' Nicolas told Carol, who found herself on his right, 'but here water is almost as precious as wine. My dear Director——' He turned to Varelle without waiting for Carol to reply. 'It seems that you hold me responsible for a wasted afternoon. But it was unthinkable that anyone should expect my fellow-Gozitans to work at carnival time.'

'Surely,' said Tony, in a drawl so casual as to be offensive, 'they all do exactly as you command?'

Nicolas drew his eyebrows together in a frown. 'Some of them are my tenants, it is true,' he said, 'but they are their own masters. We are not in the Middle Ages, here in Gozo.'

'Come now,' said Varelle. 'I have seen you, and your

tenants. They are devoted to you. You cannot claim that your wishes are not important.'

'They may have a certain respect for my wishes,' said Nicolas, 'because we have a common interest, but during the second weekend of May nothing—for me as for them—is more important than the carnival.'

Varelle shrugged his shoulders. 'And I——' he pulled a rueful face '—I had no thought that anything in the world could take precedence over the completion of my great masterpiece. But why did they not tell me themselves, yesterday, when I said to them, "Everyone will be here at eleven o'clock"?'

'They were too polite to tell you that you were wrong,' said Nicolas.

'*You* could have told me,' said Varelle. 'You would not have been too polite.'

Very true, Carol thought, remembering the afternoon of the day before. No one could accuse Nicolas of over-politeness.

'So I could,' said Nicolas, unperturbed, 'if I had not been driving all over the island looking for the wretched Madrilena.' He paused, and smiled. 'And finding you a more than adequate substitute.' His eyes met Carol's, and she did not know whether to take this as a compliment or not. The words alone were not flattering, but the look and the smile which accompanied them were appreciative, even proprietorial, Carol thought. She glanced along the table at Elaine, remembering her warning, and then firmly turned her attention to the food, which was delicious.

'How long does the merry-making last?' Tony asked, across her.

'Only two days,' Nicolas told him. 'A procession this afternoon. Traditional dances in the square this evening.

And the same tomorrow.'

Varelle clutched his forehead. 'Only two days!' he said. 'But in any event, tomorrow is Sunday, and no one would have agreed to work on a Sunday. I know this now, very well. And if I had known it at the beginning I tell you I would not have been so full of my wonderful idea of using locals for my actors. Last Sunday, for instance, I could do no more than close-ups between Madrilena and Antonio.'

'Good thing you did,' Kate said, bluntly, 'or you'd have been really in a fix.'

'It's still cheaper for you than importing plane-loads of actors,' said Nicolas. 'They will do anything you ask them on Monday.'

'I am lucky that Monday is not a saint's day,' said Varelle. 'You are a fine landowner, my friend, with your splendid irrigation schemes, and your desalination plants, and plans to make the rocks fertile, but you would never make a film director. You have no regard for overtime, or budgets, or time running out. Have you thought that you are depriving your people of double pay by not encouraging them to work on Sundays and saints' days?'

'And at carnival time? You, my dear Director, are the one who is out of touch. If they worked for you today, or tomorrow, what would they gain? Some extra pay. But they would lose much more. They would begin to lose their traditions and, worse than that, their self-respect. We do not have much wealth here in Gozo, but those two things make us, at least, partly content.'

Despite the lightness of his tone, Nicolas was serious, Carol could see.

'Only partly?' she said.

He turned to her with the intense look she found so disturbing. 'It is a very small island, too small for everything to be found here. Our people are great travellers. They go out to see the world: Australia, Canada, England perhaps. But then they come back.' He leaned forward, and spoke more earnestly than before. 'And when they come back, it is my intention that there shall always be land worth coming back for. Earth that is not wasted and barren and dry. And a spirit that is not . . . But I shall bore you.' He broke off and laughed, and began to talk of the film and the scenes yet to be shot.

He really cares, thought Carol. He cares about all the people in Gozo. He must hate to see them become mere tourist attractions, sellers of straw hats and lace handkerchiefs.

She found herself watching his face, comparing him with Varelle. The two men were different from one another in every way. She was amused to see how the volatile director gradually succumbed to the charm of his surroundings—or was it the charm of his host? And Nicolas, as host at his own table, was more relaxed than she had yet seen him. Listening to Varelle, he was perfectly still, wasting no energy on unnecessary movement, while the other talked with every part of himself. Varelle's head turned from side to side; his eyes flickered; his hands spread wide; his beard tipped to the ceiling when he laughed; his shoulders hunched as he made a point.

It gave Nicolas a look of added strength. Sitting there, leaning back in his chair, his silence was not an acceptance of Varelle's views, but an appraisal of them. His stillness was not passive. There was an element of danger in it, and power. Carol pitied anyone who tried to cross swords with him. She wondered about the brides-to-be. Tony had said there were three, but he was probably exaggerating. Even if there had been one, what could she have been like, and why had she never become a bride?

At that moment, Nicolas lifted his head and caught Carol's gaze fixed on him. Although she looked down at once at the pear she was peeling, she was very conscious of the fact that she had been staring at him, and that he knew it.

'Well?' Nicolas said. 'And are you angry with me, too?'

'Why?' said Carol, who had been too absorbed in her thoughts to follow the talk going on round her. 'Should I be?'

'For breaking my word,' said Nicolas. 'I promised that you would be free in a day, two at the most.'

'So you did,' said Carol, thinking how little it seemed to matter now whether she went home on the Monday, or the day after, or indeed until the following week. Her work was safely done; her studio could be trusted to produce the samples for Célie et Cie. She was in no hurry. She had no intention of being swept out of her emotional depth by such a dangerously attractive man as Nicolas, but surely there could be no harm in allowing herself to enjoy his company.

'In any case,' Nicolas was saying, 'it would have been a pity for you to miss the carnival.'

'When does it begin?' Carol asked, thinking how typical was his calm assumption that she would like whatever he thought was good for her.

'At four,' he said, 'but everyone prepares for at least two hours before.'

'And where is the best place to see the procession from?' she said. John and Rosie would have loved it. A super home movie subject, John would have said, and they would have shown it to their friends, along with the shots of Rosie water-skiing and John walking along the beach in his fisherman's hat. She wondered if they would be home by now, and then realised with a slight shock that they could not be. So much time seemed to have gone by since she waved goodbye to them that very morning.

She looked up and saw Nicolas leaning back in his chair with a look of amusement. 'If,' he said, 'you are wishing that your brother and your friend could have been here to see the carnival, I cannot agree.'

'Oh?' said Carol, hoping that he could not read all her thoughts so easily.

'No,' said Nicolas, without explaining further. 'And the best place to be——' he smiled at her in the sure knowledge that she would agree with him '—is with me.'

CHAPTER THREE

CAROL knew that if she lived to be a hundred she would never forget that Saturday. Later, she was to try to make herself believe that Nicolas had set out to charm her, deliberately, with calculated and typical ruthlessness, but at the time it was an afternoon and evening of sheer magic.

It began ordinarily enough. The lunch party came to an end, with Varelle giving long and involved orders to his cameramen, and then deciding that he would go with them to pick out the best spots for filming the procession. 'I can use this for the credits,' he said. 'Kate, you come with me.'

That left Tony, Elaine, Nicolas and Carol. They did not sit long over coffee. Elaine kept up an aloof silence, and Tony was ill at ease with his host, who made little effort to entertain him.

When they did go, Nicolas made it clear to the other two that he had room in his car for only one passenger, and that one was to be Carol. As he held the door of the Land Rover for Elaine, Carol caught such a look of venom from those narrowed eyes as to make her wonder if it came from jealousy because Nicolas had never paid her, Elaine, any attention, or fury because he once had.

Carol forgot about it as soon as Nicolas put his own car into gear and roared away, regardless of the narrowness of the walled drive and the roughness of its surface.

'This time I shall not drive so fast,' he said, turning the car in the opposite direction to that taken by the Land Rover. Carol laughed and said she did not believe him, but

40

he kept his word, slowing down as soon as they reached the outskirts of the first little town. The road was filled with whole families walking in the same direction. Everyone was dressed in their best, the older people all in black, the young in vivid colours. But it was the children who caught Carol's attention, so white were their socks, so spick and span their clothes.

'They are beautiful!' she exclaimed once, and Nicolas answered briefly,

'They are loved. It is a good recipe for beauty.'

More than once he stopped the car, to talk to an old man standing under a tree, to greet a mother and son, to exchange words with a group of dancers who had come to rest, their huge papier mâché carnival heads set down on the ground beside them.

The halting of the car, Carol noticed, was always a signal for smiles and greetings. 'They all seem to know you,' she said after one family had gathered round, everyone talking at once in Maltese.

'Not very surprising,' Nicolas said coolly. 'My family has been at Xatahn for six hundred years. It would be strange if I were not known.'

'But have you lived all your life here?' Carol asked, with enough surprise in her voice to bring a curl of amusement to the firm line of his mouth.

'Would that be so astonishing?' he said. 'We are not quite savages here, my little tourist.' His voice changed. 'But since you have asked . . . I was sent to an English school; I went to a French university. And like all other Gozitans I have my share of wanderlust. My interests are what you might call international.'

Jetset, thought Carol, but repented at once. Jetsetters had no roots, and if one thing stood out clearly, it was that

Nicolas belonged closely, fiercely, to his own land.

'Every town has its own team of dancers,' he was saying now. 'I brought you here early to see the preparations before the grand procession starts. It does not bore you?' The last was more statement than question, but Carol answered warmly.

'Oh no! I love seeing all the floats, and the bands—does every town have a band, too?—and meeting people. Tourists don't meet people properly as a rule—only as sightseers and customers.'

'I know. Tourism is just another crop to us. And a very profitable one.'

'Plant them in hotels. Feed with food and drink and ancient temples and sunshine . . .'

Nicolas laughed. 'Like a tree,' he said. 'Then give a shake to the branches, and the money comes pouring down.'

'And when their pockets are empty?'

'Send them away. Unfortunately we can't dig them into the ground. We simply hope to plant another good crop next year.'

After this, when they stopped, Nicolas made a point of introducing Carol, not as a tourist, nor even as one of the film company, but as 'a friend from England'.

In Gozo the division between the village-sized towns and the country is sharp and sudden. At one moment the car was bumping over a narrow track of rough stones, at the next they were in among the tall houses of golden-grey stone, where a grand and ornate church cast its shadow on the crowded central square.

'Oh!' Carol said in delight. A line of decorated donkey carts was drawn up along one side of the square. 'Can we go and look?'

'Of course,' said Nicolas, amused by her enthusiasm. 'I

have promised to inspect them myself before they take their place in the procession.'

One of the donkey carts had been transformed into a Noah's Ark, another into a gingerbread house with barley sugar chimneys. A third had become a marvellous bird's nest, and a fourth was a flower basket, its handle decked with blossoms, paper flowers among the real.

The children were dressed in every colour in which crêpe paper could be bought, and with headdresses of every flower which could possibly be made from it. They were being helped into their places by the driver, his spare form clothed in a suit of shiny black. One child was so small that he was in danger of being overlooked, until Nicolas came to his rescue, lifting him gently and placing him safely inside the decorated cart.

'You like children?' she said, on a note of surprise.

'Do you mean do I like them boiled, fried, steamed or roasted alive?' he said, smiling down. 'Who has been giving me an ogre's reputation?'

'It didn't go with the image,' said Carol, remembering Tony's waspish description.

'Your image of me?' Nicolas asked. 'Or somebody else's?' A man pushing a barrow decorated with flags and paper windmills went past. He was selling what looked like white mounds of whipped egg white with a sticky almond smell.

'What is it?' Carol asked, glad of the diversion. 'Everyone under the age of ten seems to be eating it.'

'*Prinjolata,*' said Nicolas. 'Carnival cake. But remember that images are formed only in somebody's imagination.'

Carol found his gaze uncomfortably searching. 'Surely,' she said, 'you of all men don't mind what people think of you.'

'What *people* think, no,' he said. 'But you ...' He broke

off. 'It is disconcerting, but——' he laid his hand on her arm, for a moment only '—yes, *that* I do mind.'

Perhaps it was lucky that a band consisting of a clarinet, drum and tuba struck up a loud and lively march at a distance of about ten paces, so that Carol did not have to find words to cover the ridiculous leap of her heart at his touch.

As if they had been waiting for a signal, the donkey carts, dancers, floats and all the groups which had made a kaleidoscope of scattered disorder in the square, shook themselves together and became a regular procession.

'This is only a small part of the whole thing,' said Nicolas. 'No more than three districts. They form up here and march on into Xewkija to join the rest. Every district has its own band, and its float, its grotesque masks and its troupe of dancers. Stand here, by me.' It was a command, Carol observed, not a request.

They stood side by side in the centre of the square in front of a statue, while the bands marched, the floats swayed and rumbled, the donkey carts trotted, and the grotesque heads danced past.

'It's like taking the salute,' said Carol in a lull of silence between two bands. 'You expect everyone to do an eyes right when they come past.'

'There is a time for joking,' Nicolas said, half mocking, half severe. 'But this is serious. You may look impressed, or admiring, or proud, or all three together. But do not laugh.'

'I'll try,' said Carol. To see Nicolas taking part so wholeheartedly in the carnival had opened her eyes to a side of him which was new to her. So far she had seen him as a headstrong madman—that was yesterday—then as a man round whom rumour wove tales of a black past, a Bluebeard of a man. But here he was, surrounded by tumbling clowns and dancers dressed as Mickey Mouse and Donald Duck, and children holding bunches of flowers in their fists.

One of these, a small boy Carol recognised as the owner of Pietro the rabbit, threw a yellow daisy from his bunch. It landed at Nicolas's feet, and he picked it up, thanked the child with a bow and a wave, and gravely presented it to Carol. She tucked the flower into the neck of her shirt, and waved her own thanks.

As the last of the procession, Neptune's chariot drawn by green seahorses, disappeared out of the square, an old woman in black came up to Nicolas out of the crowd, and spoke to him. Carol recognised her as the lace-maker in the little house by Calypso's cave. Nicolas bent down to take both her hands in his, and the old woman, glancing at Carol, went on in English,

'And why are you not already in your place in the Grand Stadium?' There was a chiding, almost scolding tone in her voice, which Nicolas took with surprising meekness.

'You are always right, Ta Dentella. Tomorrow I shall represent the family with all due ceremony. Today I have delegated that duty to my mother. She likes to be sole ruler on the first day, and as you know there are times when she finds my presence an embarrassment.'

'She is very proud of you,' said the old woman, 'when you do not trouble her by pretending to be wilder than you are.'

Nicolas looked at Carol with an expression of mock despair. 'You see how I am misunderstood. Ta Dentella was my nurse, so she knows me better than anyone else in the whole island. To her, I am still a very small boy who has to be kept in order, and told to be good, and to behave like a gentleman.'

The old woman laughed. 'He never does what he is told.

Never. Not even when he was only as big as this . . .' And she held out her hand about three feet from the ground.

'I can believe that,' said Carol, looking at the old lace-maker with respect. She could not imagine anyone even trying to tell Nicolas what to do.

'You must not fear him,' the old woman told Carol, unexpectedly. 'He can look—oh, so bad—a warrior. I have seen him look so when he did not want to eat his *tarja*. When he was four, and like an angry tiger, he say one day that he will throw me into a dungeon and feed me on frogs and snails! But inside his heart . . . ah, that is a very different matter.'

For the first time since she had met him, Carol saw Nicolas look embarrassed.

'Ta Dentella,' he said. 'I must take Miss Goodwin away before you destroy my reputation utterly. How can I sustain my role as an ogre if you tell her what I was like when I was four?'

'Heaven bless you, all the same,' called the lace-maker after them as he hurried Carol away in the wake of the disappearing procession.

'At any moment I expected her to tell you that I was kind to animals and always said my prayers,' he said wryly.

'It's obvious that she thinks you can do no wrong,' Carol said. 'I should think she always let you have your own way from the cradle. No wonder she let you carry me off yesterday in that terribly high-handed way. She probably thought that anything you chose to do *must* be right.'

Nicolas caught her hand, and turned her to face him.

'Will you forget how we met?' he said, and there was a steely note in his voice, though he was smiling. 'And begin again? Think that we have just been introduced at a decorous lunch party, and that it is a great pleasure that you are with me——' he paused, and tightened his hold on her hand '—during the carnival.'

What a very disconcerting gaze he had, Carol thought once more. The look went on for a long time, without a word being spoken, before Nicolas turned away quickly, as if he had been searching in her eyes for something which he was almost afraid to see.

I must be careful, Carol told herself. He's much, much too attractive to fall in love with. That there was a danger of this happening she was only too well aware.

By the end of the afternoon, before the first fireworks shot into the gathering dusk, the danger was no longer a danger. It had become a fact.

Being alone with Nicolas among the crowds of people hurrying to Xewkija was somehow even more intimate than if they had been alone on a desert island. The crowd pressed them together, jostling them and then threatening to part them, so that it was quite natural for Nicolas to take her hand and hold it very firmly in his while he pushed a way through for them both to a good vantage point, overlooking the processional route.

The first band came into view, and the first of the decorated lorries lumbered past, smothered in flowers and followed by its band of leaping dancers and tumblers, while in the distance the great heads of the carnival figures lurched and swayed. A spirit of joyous intoxication filled the air. It rose from the procession—a spilling out of colour, of movement, of noise—filling Carol's eyes, and her ears, and her heart.

She could not have said at what exact time Nicolas put his arm round her shoulders, nor precisely when she became aware of the fact that he was looking at her rather than at the procession. His expression was curiously tender, as if she were a small child out on a treat. But then she caught a flash of something deeper, more intense than tenderness, as he laughed, and bent his head so close to hers that she found herself wanting him to kiss her. She was startled to find how strong this wish was.

They said little. There was no need. The afternoon passed so quickly that it was a shock to see the last of the floats, a gigantic Calypso reclining in the mouth of her flower-decked cave. As it swayed past them, Carol noticed someone waving from the other side of the route.

'Isn't that Varelle?' she said. 'And Kate—there, waving to us.'

'What a pity that we have not seen them,' said Nicolas, holding her arm firmly so that she could not wave back. 'Come, it is time to go.' And he pulled her swiftly through the throng, now beginning to surge in upon the tail of the procession.

Carol did not ask him why he had wanted to escape.

'You did not want to join them,' Nicolas told her, rather than asked, in his customary dictatorial way. 'They can do no more filming today, and there are better things to do than listen to the plans and frustrations of the good Varelle.'

As they drove away from Xewkija, Carol knew that he was right. She did not want anything to break the veil of magic which the island, in Nicolas's company, was beginning to throw over her.

It was all very different from the week before, when she and Rosie and John had been holidaymakers together. By this time of day they were usually in their hotel, having a drink, changing for dinner, writing postcards. Now she was driving along darkening, mysterious roads, beside a man she had met the day before as a tyrant, but who was now a considerate and entertaining companion.

Carol did not know if he was consciously making up for his rudeness of the previous day, or if he had undergone some subtle change of personality. It did not seem to matter. The effect was the same. She felt a heady elation which sprang both from the festival spirit of the carnival, and the excitement of being with Nicolas.

'I seem to make a habit of abducting you,' Nicolas said abruptly, turning his head. 'You don't mind.' Again he had made a statement, not asked a question. The maddening thing was that he was right. Carol did not mind; she did not mind at all.

'Where are you abducting me to this time?' she asked, lightly.

They had left the looming height of the citadel, and threaded a way through the narrow streets on the outskirts of Victoria. Behind them, fireworks were shooting their stars into the rapidly darkening sky.

'In Xlendi there is a restaurant on the water's edge,' he told her. 'If we are lucky, it will not be patronised by our friends. I took care to recommend them to another, on the far side of Gozo.'

'You don't like them much, do you?' Carol asked.

'They provide extra work for everyone,' he said. 'And money for my schemes. So they are tolerable.'

'But as individuals, you don't like them?' she persisted.

'Varelle is amusing,' he said. 'And as ruthless as I am, when it comes to getting what he wants. The good Kate keeps him in order. But the others . . .' He dismissed them with a shrug, and a change of subject.

'This valley that we're driving along—do you like it?'

'It's beautiful,' said Carol.

'It was a game reserve for the Grand Master of the Knights of St John, about three hundred years ago. The trees are beautiful, but they had a practical purpose, too.'

'Coolness?' said Carol.

'Not entirely,' said Nicolas. 'The trees were put there for the birds to live in, and the birds were there for the Knights to kill.'

'How cruel,' said Carol. 'What kinds of birds?'

'Pigeon, quail, turtle doves.'

'That makes it worse.' For a moment Elaine's warning came back to her, but only as an absurdity to be dismissed.

'The bird that rhymes with love?' said Nicolas, smiling. 'Doves can be as greedy as pigeons when they eat a farmer's crops. And nobody minds shooting pigeons. It's a profitable pursuit.'

'Like shooting pictures?' Carol put in swiftly, and he shook his head.

'Forget about the filming,' he ordered, 'Working hours are finished. Tonight you will see the island as it should be seen. Not through a tourist's viewfinder, nor through the eye of a film camera.'

Carol had been to the narrow inlet of Xlendi before, with the others, and had loved the way the water ran clear as glass over the sand, between the high-walled rocky sides of the harbour, up to the little waterfront with its row of busy quayside shops. But now the rails of sweaters had been wheeled away, and the shops were shuttered for the night. Without the constant to-and-fro of visitors and fishermen, it was touched with magic.

Everybody was away in the town, celebrating the carnival with noise and lights. Here there was quiet. All the boats were tied up, rocking silently under the brooding mass of rock on either side. There was no sound, nothing but the quiet lap of the water, and a subdued noise of pots and pans being moved about in the restaurant behind them.

The man who ran the restaurant seemed to know Nicolas well, and greeted them as if they were the two people he most wanted to see in the world. He was small, and neat, with a pointed chin and polished hair.

'Victor learned to cook from his father, who was a steward in your navy,' Nicolas told Carol. 'But if that makes you think of plum duff and custard,' he made a grimace, 'you would be mistaken.'

'I go to France, to learn,' Victor said, with smiling dignity. 'For two years and a half. But the best, I invent.'

'Is it true you never use a cookery book?' Nicolas asked, and Victor smiled and pointed to his forehead.

'This is my cookery book, Baron, sir,' he said. 'Every dish comes to me new, like a poem. Today you will have a *fritturi* of small fish which I go to choose this very afternoon, when the boat bring it. And I have some meat which is so tender and fine that the Queen of England could eat it. But I prefer to cook it for you, with a sauce made from herbs and olives, and a few other things. And while I cook, you will drink.' He produced a carafe of red wine and two glasses, and left them.

'He's right,' Nicolas said, pouring wine into Carol's glass. 'Most chefs produce quite good prose from their kitchens. But Victor is a poet. You will see.'

Carol could not tell whether it was the food, which indeed lived up to all Victor had claimed for it, or the unusually mellow Gozo wine, or the friendly charm of her host—that dangerous charm of which he had even boasted, and against which she had fully intended to be on her guard—but by the time they were drinking their coffee she felt the magic of the evening surrounding her, pressing in on her from every side.

They had talked of quite ordinary things. Carol told him about her design studio in London, her regular contracts with some of the big textile firms in Britain, and her more adventurous work for Célie et Cie, who supplied the greatest names in Paris *haute couture* and had been taking her designs for four seasons now.

'I commend you,' said Nicolas. 'You must be very good.'

'Not bad,' Carol said, with honesty. 'Good enough to be able to travel a bit when I want new ideas.'

'So I must thank the demands of high fashion for your presence here. And did you find enough inspiration in these islands?'

'More than enough for half a dozen collections!' she said.

Nicolas smiled as she told him of the sights which had fired her imagination: the pitted sandstone of the ancient temples, the fragile basketwork of the balloon-shaped fish traps, the lights shining like coloured ribbons into the dark water of Valetta's Grand Harbour, the fields of poppies and yellow daisies she had looked down on from the ramparts of the citadel.

'You have a seeing eye,' he said, with warm approval in his voice.

In return he told her of his boyhood in Gozo, of his holdings which were spread all over the island, and of the tenants who farmed them. He talked of his plans to bring an unfailing supply of water to the land, even the most barren; of the systems of irrigation which had been used for centuries past, the wells worked first by donkeys and now by windmills; and of the advanced new technology he was hoping to use in the future.

They were quite ordinary, mundane things, but the same

alchemy which had touched the little harbour, and the meal, and the quayside where they sat, was at work in themselves, too. It seemed to Carol that she and Nicolas were alone in a world of their own, a world of magic, a bubble of contentment.

No, not a bubble, she thought. Bubbles burst, and this was too real a magic to burst or leak away. It was a magic which filled the night like an incense. It stayed with them while Nicolas drove her on a moonlit tour of the island. For the moon had risen now, and this, she told herself, might have something to do with the silver enchantment of that exceptional evening.

Never had the stark outline of Fungus Rock looked more dramatic, nor the Inland Sea more mysterious. It was as if moonlight had the power to heighten everything they saw, and everything they felt, or were beginning to feel, about one another.

The strange network of salt pans cut in the rocks at Xwiena glistened with a crystal brightness they never had in the daytime. The citadel, with its great sheer walls rising black above them, had all the majesty and all the strength of the time before it had become a ruined shell, brooded over by its cathedral. Everything—the square-cut towers on the hillsides, the massive stone blocks of Ggantiga, the uncanny spider's web shape of the windmill at Qala—all were given a mystery and a power by the black and silver night.

At last, Nicolas stopped the car and they got out, to walk down a path towards the sea, a path which Carol soon realised was the one she had come up on that hot and sunny afternoon which seemed a hundred years away, in another lifetime. Yesterday.

'Isn't this . . .' she said, and stopped.

'The path to Calypso's cave,' Nicolas said. 'The mouth of the cave is blocked now. A fall of rock. No one can come out or go in.'

They came to the half-built villa, with its statues and flower-filled urns casting moon shadows on to the broad paving stones of the terrace. Nicolas led Carol through the blank doorway, and between the pillars of a roofless courtyard, and out again to the terrace which overlooked the bay.

'Whose house is it?' Carol asked. 'Will there be somebody living here?'

'It was begun seven years ago, when ...' Nicolas hesitated, and went on, 'as a summer house.'

'Why was it never finished?' Carol asked.

'It will be,' Nicolas said, explaining nothing. 'Do you like it?'

Carol looked down at the wide curving beach of sand, white now in the moonlight, and the near-black sea, its surface broken by ripples of silver. The smell of thyme and fennel wafted up from the hillside, for the air was warm.

'It's peaceful, and ...' she searched for a word to express the magical quality of that peacefulness, 'spellbinding.'

'Spellbinding?' Nicolas laughed, and it was a laugh she could feel, like a caress. 'Calypso cast a spell on Ulysses, the legend goes, which kept him here for seven years.' His eyes were on her face, unwavering, dark, compelling.

'It would have been for ever, if he hadn't been so strong-minded,' said Carol.

'For ever,' repeated Nicolas. 'For ever is a long time. They would have still been here, standing where you and I are standing.'

He took both her hands in his, and the warmth from his touch went through her whole body.

Carol wished that she did not feel so light-headed when she looked up at him, that her heart would not beat quite so fast, and that her voice was not so breathless as she answered,

'Seeing what we are seeing, hearing what we are hearing.'

The moon made the black sea into a silver mirror. A single sea bird called. The small sound of waves sidling on to the sand came like a whisper from the beach below.

'They would not have stood for so long,' Nicolas said.

Swiftly, he bent to kiss her, and the night enfolded them in its magic, as in a black and silver cloak.

CHAPTER FOUR

THE only trouble about magic, Carol thought as she opened her eyes the next morning, is that it does not last. She lay in the narrow bunk of the caravan which had been Madrilena's, and thought about Nicolas with a strong mixture of happiness and regret.

She could still feel the intense pleasure of being in his arms, his mouth hard and fierce on hers, his body taut and strong as he held her against him. She remembered the way he had looked at her, compelling, insistent, and his laugh as she eventually struggled to free herself.

Why had she struggled? Why, when all she wanted in the world was to give way to the flood of emotions which threatened to overcome her? Naïveté? Instinct? Rebellion? Caution? Her stupid schoolgirl Englishness?

Nicolas had laughed, kissed her once more with a thoroughness which took her breath away, and let her go.

Carol did not as a rule allow herself to indulge in daydreams about the men who at various times had come into her life. Not that there had been many, certainly none who had counted for anything. Absolutely none at all like Nicolas. No one had ever roused in her any of the longings which Nicolas's kisses had stirred up.

And Nicolas? How had he felt about yesterday, that golden afternoon, the black and silver evening? That they had been no more than an entertainment? An amusing interlude? Remembering the look in his eyes when he said goodbye, Carol found herself drifting into that perilous

daydreaming state of mind where anything was possible—
love, for instance, and being with Nicolas not for one day,
or a week, but for a lifetime.

A brisk knock on the door broke into this dangerous
reverie, and Kate appeared with a mug of tea and a wide
smile.

'I know it's Sunday,' she said, 'but Varelle wants to
rehearse.'

She sat on the edge of the bed and gazed round her, at the
neatly stacked luggage, just as it had been brought up from
the hotel, at the dressing-table, bare except for a crumpled
yellow flower.

'No need to ask if you enjoyed the carnival,' she said. 'We
caught a glimpse of you, more than once.'

'I didn't see you,' said Carol, holding the mug in front of
her face to hide the smile which she could not check.

'I'm not surprised,' Kate said. 'You both looked fairly
preoccupied. Almost starry-eyed, in fact.'

'Nonsense,' Carol said. 'Nicolas was very interesting. He
was telling me about farming, and crops, and so on. Did
you know they grow peaches and figs and vines, as well as
potatoes and tomatoes?'

'Most romantic,' said Kate. 'Tomatoes were called love-
apples once, weren't they?'

'What were you saying about rehearsing?' Carol asked
her. She did not mean to discuss love in any form.

'Oh, yes—the wedding ceremony in the chapel on the
cliff,' Kate said. 'And the wedding procession coming up
from the harbour. Not a dress rehearsal, just the
movements. Nothing to worry about.'

But to Carol, with Varelle standing over her like a
ringmaster cracking his whip, it seemed that there was
everything to worry about. The simplest actions—walking,

standing, turning—had become as complicated as grand ballet.

'No, no, no!' he shouted at her. 'Not like that. Not as if you are going on a quick march. Slowly, *slowly*. Remember this is a forced marriage. You do not know he is your childhood lover. Not yet. You cannot see him through the veil, and your eyes are cast down. Now, try again. Draw back. Turn away from Antonio. No! Not your back on him. A half turn, and when he takes your hand to put on the ring, drag it away. Turn again. Lower your head. Don't look at the priest! Don't smile—why are you smiling?'

'I didn't know I was,' said Carol, by now so flustered that she could hardly tell what she was doing.

'What is that on your face, then?' Varelle demanded, dancing with rage. 'A grimace? A grin? Take it off. I do not want a smile. I want tears! I want terror! I want every movement of your body to be a protest against the terrible thing that is happening. And what do I have? A pudding! A puppet! A doll!'

'I did tell you I couldn't act,' Carol said 'Right at the beginning.'

'Act? Act!' said Varelle, more furious with every word. 'I do not want you to *act*. I want you to *be*.' He dropped his voice. 'Is it so much to ask?' he said. 'You must feel. Bah! Must I throw snakes at you to make you show fear?'

'I'm sorry,' said Carol. 'I'm doing my best. It's just that having everybody all round . . .'

'It's nerves,' said Tony. 'Varelle, you'll make it worse if you shout at her. Look, my sweet, just remember that I'm the last person you want to marry, but there's a Turkish sailor with a scimitar guarding your Mum and Dad and three little brothers and baby sister, and just do what comes naturally. You'll be perfect.'

Carol tried to follow his advice, and by mid-morning Varelle had stopped shouting at her and tearing his hair, and seemed to be grudgingly satisfied.

'One hundred per cent more panic,' he said, 'and you will pass. Panic, and protest. Go away and practise. Antonio will coach you.'

But as things turned out, Tony could not coach her. It was while they were driving in procession down the steep rocky zig-zag to the little harbour that the accident happened.

Tony, who was driving the leading car, took the last bend much too fast; the wheels skidded and the car turned over, throwing its occupants, Tony and Carlos and one of the cameramen, out on the hillside before it rolled over and over to crash thunderously on the rocks below.

Carol was with Kate and Elaine in the Land Rover behind, and saw it happen like a scene in slow motion: Tony, flung in the air and landing awkwardly with one leg doubled beneath him; the look of alarm on the face of his fellow actor before he, too, hit the ground; the cameraman rolling, curled up like a parachutist.

He was lucky, picking himself up at once, but Carlos lay like a crumpled rag doll, alarmingly still and white. Tony, when they reached him, was trying to sit up, but fell back with a groan.

'Don't move him!' Varelle sprayed orders in all directions. 'Run back! Ring for a doctor! An ambulance. Tell them we have one wounded, and one—— He is so pale—is he dead?'

The actor Carlos was not dead, but unconscious. He was taken away to the hospital in Victoria as soon as the ambulance team arrived. Tony, too, went to the hospital, Varelle with him. When the director came back, alone, he was pale not with worry but with anger.

'A broken leg!' He threw out his hands. 'It would happen to me!'

'I thought it had happened to poor Tony,' said Kate.

'Yes, yes. I know. And I feel sorry for him—very sorry,' Varelle said dismissively. 'But for him it is only a broken leg. It will mend before his next picture It is I—I, Varelle—who suffer. It is not enough that I have a leading lady who vanishes, and a carnival which holds up my work for two days, at colossal inconvenience. Now, now that I am so nearly at the end, in a moment of idiocy—for he was driving like a maniac, you saw!—all at one blow, I have no leading man. To lose one star is bad. To lose two . . . Must I give it all up, after so much struggle?'

Kate tried to soothe him, but Varelle brushed her aside.

'Leave me. You are all idiots! Dolts! Imbeciles! It is the fate of a genius to be the only one who can see what is to be done. It is I who must think for us all, I, Varelle . . .'

He clapped his hands and ordered, 'Everyone away! Away from my sight. I must think alone; I must suffer alone.' He struck his forehead with one fist, and strode off, one hand behind his back.

'Just like Napoleon,' Kate whispered to Carol as they retreated. 'Don't worry. We usually let him rave a bit. It does him good, and he'll come up with the answer when he's cooled down.'

'You sound as if you're used to setbacks,' said Carol. Kate was as calm as Varelle had been frenzied.

'They happen,' said Kate. 'Every time. This is nothing to last year, when we were in Sicily. He wanted a storm. There was no wind for three weeks—unheard of at that time of year. A camera fell into a volcano—dormant, but all the same . . .'

'Wasn't that the time,' said Elaine, 'that the second female lead—you remember her, Kate—liaised too well with the press and pinched all the headlines? And that actor, the one we called Stonehenge—Varelle tried everything short of murder to get him to move one of his pre-set concrete face muscles.'

'Surprising how it all comes out in the wash,' said Kate. 'When you see the finished product up there on the big screen, all glossy and splendid, you'd never know there'd been all this backstage drama.'

As they made their way back to the line of caravans, the faint sounds of town bands were wafted to them from the inner part of the island, and Carol remembered the magic of the day before. Yesterday she had been with Nicolas, caught up in the sights and sounds of the carnival. Today he would be sitting formally in the stadium, in the place reserved for the Baron of Xatahn.

As if to echo her thoughts, Elaine said, with her malicious drawl, 'Look, the *grand seigneur* himself. We *are* honoured.'

Carol turned to see Nicolas's red car shoot through the gates of the film unit in a spray of dust. Before her racing heart had a chance to subside, he had disengaged his tall form from the driving seat and was striding to where they stood.

He had heard about the accident, and had come to see what could be done. 'Where's the director?' he asked Kate abruptly, but she had no need to answer. Varelle had heard the red car, and now came hurrying towards them, with outstretched arms and an exultant smile.

'My friend!' he exclaimed. 'You arrive as I arrive also at the solution to my problem. And what problems I have, in this island of yours, so full of disappearing tricks! First Madrilena, then the extras, and now Antonio. Poor

Antonio.' He put on a grave face and replaced it at once
with a look of jubilation. 'And then I think of a brilliant
solution, because, you understand, it is given to geniuses
such as Varelle to have these *coups de foudre*, brainwaves
which come out of the air like thunderbolts!'

He paused for effect. Nicolas caught Carol's eye and
smiled.

'And what is your thunderbolt?' he said. 'How do you
solve your problem?'

'Can you not guess?' Varelle cried, almost dancing in an
ecstasy of self-admiration. 'I have need of one man to play
the scenes which must be played before the film can be
finished. A tall man, with dark colouring, saturnine, a
commanding figure with the bearing of a man who is used
to power and is not afraid of danger. Can you not guess who
this man shall be, my friend?'

'No,' said Nicolas, still smiling, but stiffly. 'Who can he
be?'

'Who other but yourself?' Varelle exclaimed, throwing
his arms wide in his familiar gesture of triumph. 'Why did I
not think of it before? Why did not you, Kate, think of it?
Or you, Elaine? Why is it always left to me to have these
strokes of inspiration?'

Carol was watching Nicolas. She saw the amusement in
his eyes as he realised what Varelle wanted, and the iron-
hard set of his mouth as he shook his head.

'You take a great deal for granted,' he said, and there was
an ironic note in his voice which did not escape Carol,
though it had no effect upon Varelle.

'But no, my dear Nick, I do not. You will be as good as
Antonio, possibly even better. With you, it will be the real
thing. You are of the country. Your ancestors may have
been the very people who enacted this drama in real life.

What could be more fitting?'

'And if I do not agree?' Nicolas said, looking down at Varelle from his great height.

'But you will. Of course you will agree!' said Varelle, his face darkening at the very thought of his plans being crossed. 'You want the film unit to leave your beautiful island. You are as anxious for the film to be finished as I am, its director. And besides,' he went on, as Nicolas tried to speak, 'you know as well as I that if I cannot complete the film happily and successfully, I shall not be able to pay you the money which you need so badly for your great schemes for the land.'

There was a silence. Nicolas's eyebrows were drawn together in a frown of displeasure. 'You are a crook, Varelle,' he said. 'A moral blackmailer.'

They stood like two antagonists in a duel. Carol watched them, thinking that Varelle had as much chance of winning the battle of wills as a sparrow against a hawk.

'You forget that I am no actor,' Nicolas said softly, and there were six hundred years of family pride in his voice.

Varelle pointed his beard to heaven and spoke with exasperation.

'And nor is Carol an actress,' he said. 'But do I, the great Varelle, complain about such a small detail? My dear Nicolas, two days ago you were persuading Carol here that she would be doing you a great personal favour if she would agree to take part in my film. Surely you cannot refuse to do the very thing that you were asking her to do. Carol, my dear child, tell him that if he does not agree then he must be the most unreasonable man in the whole of the Mediterranean.'

Nicolas looked at Carol, his frown deepening. With that frown, Carol thought again, his nickname of Satan was apt.

'I can't tell Nicolas what to do,' she said. 'If he wants to help you, he will.'

As she spoke, she knew that she wanted him to say yes. The idea of playing the two scenes with Nicolas rather than Tony by her side gave her a feeling of sudden excitement. She lowered her head, and then, as the silence continued, raised her eyes to find Nicolas looking at her with an expression of amusement. His face had relaxed. The frown was gone, and he laughed.

'Sauce for the gander?' he said. 'I give in. I have no choice. But now, at this very moment, they are waiting for me to give the signal for the procession to begin. And tonight there is a banquet at which tradition demands that the Baron and the Baroness of Xatahn both preside. So, my dear Varelle, until tomorrow. And Carol . . .' As his eyes met hers, Carol wondered if he, too, remembered the magic of the evening before, '. . . tomorrow, it seems that I am doomed to play an unwilling groom to your reluctant bride.'

Varelle was delighted. Kate was pleased. 'He will be better than Tony. More presence.'

Only Elaine was spiteful. 'Thinks he's too good for us,' she said. 'The grand Baron slumming it among the strolling players.' When Carol tried to defend the absent Nicolas, Elaine looked sideways at her and murmured that it was a shame to see her falling for his obvious charm.

'It's only that I can't bear to see it made so easy for him with everyone—and I do mean everyone. Not Kate, of course—she's too ordinary, but Madrilena . . .' Elaine let her voice trail away, leaving Carol to imagine the rest: the candle-lit dinner by the harbour, for instance, the sightseeing by moonlight, the villa overlooking the black and silver sea.

I don't believe it, Carol said fiercely to herself. I won't believe it. But aloud she said, 'Everyone? You, too?'

The green eyes flickered as Elaine answered. 'He tried. Of course he tried.' She smiled as if at a secret memory. 'But I know a shark when I see one.' She laughed, a small rather high laugh, and Carol wonderd if the trouble with Nicolas, in Elaine's eyes, was that he had not bothered to try.

If Elaine's motive in warning Carol had been to lessen the attraction between her and Nicolas, she was a bad judge of human nature. Everyone knows, Carol thought crossly, as she tried to go to sleep that night, that the effect of warning you against a man is to make him doubly attractive.

She did not sleep well. Her dreams were a jumble of disasters: her dress not ready, the ring lost, the priest on crutches, Tony and Nicolas continually changing places, the cliff giving way as the ring was placed on her finger, a deep ravine dividing her from Nicolas.

So vivid was her dream that in the morning she asked Kate about the part of the priest. They had all been so anxious about Tony's part that she had quite forgotten that of the third actor in the scene.

The news of the casualties was encouraging. Tony was in plaster, and due to fly back to England as soon as he was allowed to travel. Carlos was out of his concussion, with cuts and bruises and an immensely swollen black eye.

'He can't possibly do the part,' Kate said. 'He looks horrific, and he's been ordered complete rest. If Nicolas can't find someone, it'll be one of the more presentable extras, I suppose. How are you feeling? No butterflies, I hope.'

'None to speak of,' Carol said. But by the time she had been dressed in the heavy brocade wedding dress, and after the lengthy ordeal of having her face scraped and smoothed and made up, and her hair pushed tightly under the black wig, she was feeling far more nervous than she cared to admit.

The last thing she wanted was to make a fool of herself before so many people: not only the three hundred extras who were gathered and waiting to descend the hillside, but the camera crew, the other actors, Varelle, and of course Nicolas. Nicolas, looking perfectly at ease in Tony's costume, greeted Carol with a gleam of appreciative amusement in his eyes.

'Very becoming,' he said. 'Any man would be proud to be given such a bride. You even succeed in looking tremulous.'

Carol smiled briefly. 'You don't know how scared I am,' she said. 'What if I trip over these long skirts? Varelle will kill me.'

'I promise not to let him eat you,' said Nicolas gravely, and Carol laughed, and tried to relax.

Even so, by the time they were all in position down at the harbour, Carol was sure that no bride had ever felt half as nervous as she did at that moment. She tried to steady herself by the knowledge that her face was hidden under the heavy lace veil. Nicolas, standing beside her, was a tall, reassuring figure, powerfully still. Varelle, on the other hand, was fizzing with energy and last-minute instructions.

'Only one take of this,' he said. 'There is no second chance. It must be without fault. I do not want to march my three hundred up to the top over and over again when they have made their descent.'

And to Carol, 'Keep your eyes on the ground. Hold up your skirts, but not too much. And when you draw aside from the road at the third bend, halfway up, to let the torrent of people rush down past you, turn your head to follow them. They are your people. They are being driven away. You cannot bear to see them go. And when you continue, it is with a reluctant step, as if you would put off the hour of your marriage for ever. It is a very terrible thing for you, this marriage.'

Carol tried to think how terrible it would be, but found it hard. Walking slowly beside Nicolas, almost as close as they had been on the day of the carnival, she had a vivid memory of the moment when he had taken her face in his hands, and smoothed back her hair, and looked at her, all among the scent of the wild thyme, with the waves whispering below on the sand. It struck her that she could think of no more wonderful fate than to be married to such a man. Strong but kind. Hot-tempered but passionate. Dictatorial, but gentle, too.

Holding the folds of her skirts with care, she made an effort to concentrate on Varelle's instructions, but she was all too conscious of Nicolas. What were his thoughts, she wondered. Was he, too, remembering the magic of that night? Or had it been as Elaine had hinted, the sport of one evening? No more than a casual interlude in his life—easily undertaken and as easily forgotten? Or was he simply counting the hours to the time when they would all be gone, when the film would be finished and the whole tedious business at an end?

Her foot hit a stone, and for a moment she stumbled. Then she felt the warm pressure of Nicolas's hand under her elbow, and remembered just in time not to look up into his face.

'You must not look at him,' Varelle had said. 'Not until you are married do you see that he is the lover you thought you would never see again.'

At the word 'lover', she remembered, Nicolas had looked across at her and smiled. It was a smile which seemed to join them together, a thread of intimacy which no one else could see, but which she could feel, tightly strung between them. And now, if there was one thing Carol longed to see at that moment, it was Nicolas's face. She wanted to see if the look in his eyes matched the warmth of his steadying hand.

It was then they met what Varelle had called his river of human misery, streaming down towards them, forcing the small wedding party off the road, where a great boulder stood as a marker. The crowd poured down past them, screaming and wailing, driven by Turkish sailors with great curved swords.

Carol could not imagine what six thousand would have sounded like. Three hundred were frightening enough, and she was glad they had reached the bend in the road where the boulder stood in time, for otherwise she thought they must have been swept off their feet and crushed in the headlong stampede.

Not that it was much of a haven, Carol discoverd, when she unwisely glanced down and behind her. They were standing on a platform of rock almost overhanging the sea, so steeply did the cliff drop away beneath. And although they had climbed no more than a third of the way up the road, the sight of the waves breaking on the rocks below was quite enough to make Carol feel dizzy with fear. She clutched at Nicolas's sleeve with a hand which shook.

The response from Nicolas was instant. His hand came down over hers with such strength, such power, that she felt all at once safe, relieved, and immeasurably happy.

'Not afraid?' she heard him say in a low voice.

'Of course not!' she said, and then added, more honestly, 'Not now.'

Carol heard him laugh under his breath, and then the crowds were past, and the small wedding party set itself once more upon the upward path. Varelle, beside himself with self-congratulation, ordered them to stop.

'Enough!' he cried. 'It will be a magnificent sequence! My dear Nick, I could make of you a fine actor. And Carol . . . ah, Carol, if you could appear a little more desolated, I would say you were not bad, not bad at all. And when the last scene is done, the marriage in the chapel, I shall breathe again.'

'It was a real chapel, you know,' Kate told Carol while the three girls ate sandwiches in the shade of Kate's caravan. Varelle had swept Nicolas off with him for last-minute instructions—'no more rehearsal, we finish today,'—but had grudgingly allowed a thirty-minute lunch break. Carol wished that she could have taken off the tight, hot black wig as well as the veil and gloves which she had left, thankfully, on Kate's bed.

'Thirteenth-century, one of the earliest. There used to be hundreds of them. Every well-to-do family put one up, and endowed it as a sort of thanks-offering to their own patron saint.'

'What a busy little researcher you are,' said Elaine.

'What happened to them all?' Carol asked.

'Pillaged by sea pirates,' said Kate, 'or fell into ruins when a bigger church was built. Then the Bishop of Gozo would come along and condemn it, until someone collected enough money to do the repairs. Then it could be re-blessed.'

'Was this one ever condemned?' Carol asked.

'I didn't find it in the records,' Kate said. 'Some of them weren't.'

'Fascinating,' said Elaine, with her lazy drawl. 'So Carol might go to church as Carol Goodwin, and come back the new Baroness of Xatahn.'

'You'd need an ordained priest first,' said Kate, crushingly.

'Who *is* playing the priest?' said Carol. 'Did Varelle find someone himself in the end? Or did he leave it to Nicolas?'

'One of the locals, I think,' said Elaine. 'And I must tell you, I heard some great gossip yesterday. Did you know that our proud and noble Baron was once jilted? Left at the altar, no less, or something like it.'

'Who told you?' said Kate.

'One of the extras. It's practically island legend by now.'

No wonder he hadn't wanted to stand in for Tony, thought Carol, and felt a stab of pity. It would have been a terrible blow to his pride. If it was true, of course. It was the kind of gossip Elaine would enjoy.

Kate jumped to her feet. 'Carol, it's time to hide away under your veil again. And don't forget, you take off the glove just before the ring goes on your finger.'

Although Carol had rehearsed every action in detail, over and over again, with Tony, she discovered that with Nicolas it was all very different. Tony had not looked at her with such intensity. He had not made her heart beat faster, nor had he given her the feeling that they were two people cut off from the rest of the world, drawn together by some magnetic force. Nicolas did all these things, and more. It was with the greatest difficulty that Carol reminded herself that she was supposed to be going to a hated wedding as an unwilling bride.

The cameras were at the back of the reconstructed chapel, with Varelle behind them. There was no congregation, the Turkish sailors having formed an escort only as far as the chapel doors, so that Carol and Nicolas stood alone before the actor who played the priest.

He was a good actor, Carol noticed, so good he might almost have been the real thing. As he spoke the old Latin words of the marriage service over them, Carol could feel rather than see Nicolas's tall, unmoving figure beside her. They stood as close together as two people can who are not actually touching one another, and Carol wished she knew what he was feeling.

The time was coming when he would have to put the wedding ring on her finger, and she knew that it would take all her powers of self-control not to look up at his face then, to see the expression in his eyes.

She had practised taking off her left glove many times until she could do it without a hitch. But this time, as she did so, her fingers felt something hard and flat, with corners, tucked into the wrist—a label, perhaps, which had worked loose. It fell into the palm of her right hand, and Carol, looking down, was amazed to see that it was a small piece of white paper, with words written on it in capital letters. They were small, but clear and legible.

The voice of the priest droned on, and Carol read the words on the slip of paper in her hand, hidden under the veil which hung round her like a bell.

'THE PRIEST IS ORDAINED,' she read. 'THE MARRIAGE WILL BE VALID.'

It's a joke, was her first thought, a joke in very bad taste. She crumpled the tiny square of paper and let it drop to the ground. But who in the world would want to play such a joke? The actor-priest? Varelle? Elaine? There was no point in it.

If only she understood Latin, she would know whether he

had yet come to the final words which pronounced them man and wife. No, that must come after the ring, with the joining of hands. 'Let no man put asunder' was the sentence which raced through her mind.

Suppose it was not a joke, but a warning? If the priest was a real priest, then he would never agree to perform a genuine marriage service as a joke. Nicolas's hand on her wrist came as a jarring shock. He was drawing her nearer to him, so that he could place the ring upon her gloveless finger.

Feverishly, she tried to think. If the priest was not marrying them as a joke, then it must be that he was doing it in all seriousness, by a pre-arranged plan. With whom?

Nicolas's grip on her wrist tightened, and Carol tried to draw her hand away, while her thoughts galloped on. Varelle hadn't engaged him, Kate had said so. It would have to be Nicolas, Nicolas himself, who had planned it.

Carol had no time to work out why. 'Big Bad Nicolas,' Tony had called him. 'Be careful how you deal with a man like the Baron of Xatahn,' Elaine had warned.

But he couldn't have planned the accident to Tony. Or could he? Her mind was in utter confusion. Dreaming about the prospect of being married to Nicolas was one thing. The reality of finding herself married to him, without her consent, for what reason she did not know, and by a ruse which showed cunning rather than love, was something altogether different. If only she had time to think!

'*In nomine Patris . . .*' the priest was saying. He raised his hands in blessing. Nicolas was holding the ring in his hand—she saw the gleam of gold—and holding her left hand in his with such a firm grasp that Carol could not pull her hand away.

For a small, suspended moment of eternity she stood there, frozen with doubt and alarm, not knowing what she should, could or would do. And then, as she felt Nicolas begin to push the ring on her finger, she tried to wrench her hand out of his, beating at him with her free hand, and crying 'No!' in a voice of frenzy.

'Before God!' Nicolas's voice cut through her like a sword, and the grip of his hand on her wrist remained as unyielding as if it had been an iron clamp. With fingers as hard and unbending as his will, he forced the band of gold down on to her finger. For an instant the priest paused in his intoning, and Carol threw all her strength into her efforts to twist away from Nicolas and escape.

But with a jerk he pulled her round almost to face him, and seizing both her hands held them so fast that she could not move. The priest's voice began again, and in a panic-stricken moment of fright and horror Carol felt his hands touch both hers and Nicolas's, and declared them irrevocably, for ever, and without question, man and wife.

Nicolas released her. Carol gazed down at her left hand, at the band of gold on her finger. The words of the priest faded. A fuzzy blackness closed in about her, and she felt herself falling, falling . . .

CHAPTER FIVE

WHEN Carol came to herself again, she was lying on the ground with Nicolas kneeling beside her, looking into her face—but whether with astonishment at her performance or concern at her collapse she could not tell. She knew that the veil must have been lifted from her face, or she would not have been able to see Nicolas at all, to see the unguarded expression in his eyes, an expression which she could not read.

Far away, as if at the end of a long tunnel, she heard Varelle exclaim, 'Stop the cameras! Carol, that was splendid. Better than I dared to hope. Real panic—one would have thought you were *effrayée*, and the fainting—a beautiful touch. It will never come better than that. It is the end. You can all go home.' And his voice faded as he turned away in a whirl of congratulations and instructions.

Carol saw Nicolas draw away as she sat up, and it was Kate who helped her to her feet, and bustled about her, cheerfully talking, as if nothing out of the ordinary had happened.

'Jolly good,' she said. 'Better than the real thing.'

'I didn't mean to faint,' said Carol, weakly.

'Stroke of genius,' said Kate. 'Solved all that silly business of throwing back the veil and looking into each other's eyes—much more effective for Nicolas to be gazing down at you. The cameras zoomed in to your face, but not too close, and then "Cut!". I've never seen Varelle more delighted.'

Kate went on chattering, but Carol hardly heard her. Sick and dizzy as she was, she had only one thought pounding in her head, as the scene that she and Nicolas had enacted came back to her. She and Nicolas—were they married? The ring—she looked at her hand. She remembered the force with which he had driven it down over her finger. The priest—where was the priest?

'The priest!' she said, interrupting Kate's enthusiastic flow. 'The man who played the priest. Where is he?' If she could be reassured that he was only an actor, after all, then it would not matter who had written the note; it might have been a stupid trick, not a warning. Once she had seen the actor, and proved he was an actor, then she could stop worrying. She would be all right.

'The priest who took Carlos's place?' said Kate. 'I don't know. Getting paid, I expect.'

'Please go and find him,' said Carol. 'It's important.'

'Why do you want to find him so badly?' Kate asked, and Carol did not dare to tell her. She could not embark upon the story of the note in her glove. Had she imagined the whole thing? Was the heat so oppressive that it had given her some kind of waking nightmare? She went to look at the exact spot before the altar where she had been standing, but there was nothing there now. Her head began to swim, and she swayed, recovered, and apologised.

'I'm sorry. I feel . . .'

'You look pretty groggy,' said Kate, worried. 'Let's have that wig off for a start. It's enough to give anyone a headache. And undo some of those tight fastenings. You ought really to be lying down, but I can't think where.

Everyone's packing up and getting ready for the off. Your caravan's in use as the paying-out desk, I'm afraid. Oh, Nick, look—she's not in very good shape.'

Carol, pressing her hands to her temples in an effort to stop the headache which was clamping an iron band round them, was only dimly aware of Nicolas's tall figure beside her. She heard his strangely detached voice telling Kate to leave it to him, he would look after everything; felt herself being picked up as if she were a sick child and then deposited on the seat of a car with a cushion under her head; and shut her eyes while somebody—she supposed it was Nicolas—started the engine.

She tried to think of nothing at all, with such success that she did not wonder where he was taking her, or realise where she was, even when the car stopped and she was lifted out and carried, in Nicolas's arms, through an arched gateway, across a courtyard with a fountain playing, and into a house she vaguely recognised, but could not place. She noticed only the calm darkness of the shuttered room, the coolness of the marble floor, and the gentle movement of a fan high in the lofty ceiling.

Only when she was lying back in a long bamboo day bed covered with soft cushions was she fully aware that Nicolas was standing over her with a very determined set to his mouth; there was no warmth in his eyes.

'There is no one here,' he said, as Carol looked about her, recognising the furniture, realising that she was in the *palazzo* of Xatahn. 'The servants are in their own quarters; they are preparing their evening meal. My mother is in her town house in Victoria. We are quite alone.'

Carol tried to sit up, and fell back against the cushions, her head throbbing.

His face softened slightly as he looked down at her. She was still wearing the sixteenth-century wedding dress, and although Kate had loosened the tight bodice, the stiff brocade was heavy and stifling, imprisoning her, weighing her down as if it were a suit of armour.

'I thought it best to bring you here,' he said. 'There were too many people about for an explanation.'

Explanation? He had said 'explanation'.

Carol looked up at him, and wondered muzzily how he could hope to explain away what he had done. How could anyone explain a forced marriage—a marriage by trickery—to someone who until last week had been a total stranger?

But if he were offering her an explanation, it must mean that he had arranged just that; that it had indeed been a planned operation, that he had seized his opportunity, and for some fantastic, extraordinary reason of his own tricked her into becoming his wife.

But why? Why had he done it? He could not have done it for love. That was plain to see from the grim expression on his face. It was as antagonists that they now faced one another, enemies. Elaine's words came back to her: 'Left at the altar, no less.' Could it be a case of revenge—revenge against one woman for what another had done to him?

Why did he stand there, so silent, looking at her? She ought to hate him. She ought to be furious at the way he had taken her life into his hands, as if it were some piece of property he had decided to buy—no, seize—against its owner's will.

But even as she looked up at him, she found that it was not easy, even now, to hate Nicolas. It did not seem to matter what he had done, nor why he had done it in such a high-handed way, nor what was to happen now. She could not feel anger or resentment. Instead, she was overcome by a great weariness. She could do no more puzzling, no more guessing, or wondering. She would listen to Nicolas, and the explanation he had brought her to Xatahn to hear. If only her tired mind could take it in, at least she would know ...

'Well?' His voice sounded, for once, like a question and, as Carol wondered why, he went on, impatience hardening the edge of his words.

'I am waiting.'

'*You* are waiting!' Carol was roused from her tiredness to answer with a flash of anger. What did he mean?

'For what? Waiting for what?' was all she could say.

'This is not a game I would advise you to play with me,' Nicolas said, his mouth as grim as she had ever seen it, his eyes hard. 'An explanation is necessary between us. And without further fencing, my dear bride, it is your explanation which I am waiting for.' He smiled, but there was no vestige of a smile in his eyes.

'Mine?' Carol said, her voice rising in astonishment.

'Yes,' said Nicolas. 'Of this.' He held out his hand. In his palm was a crumpled scrap of paper. Smoothing it out, he read, in a flat, expressionless voice, 'The priest is ordained. The marriage is valid.'

'The paper,' said Carol. 'The message.'

'Exactly,' said Nicolas. 'The message, confirming your arrangements. How you did it, or why—what evil demon possessed you to think of such a scheme—I cannot begin to imagine. If it was to pay me back for our first meeting...' He stopped, and clenched one fist in a gesture of disbelief. 'No. That I cannot believe. But why?'

Carol shut her eyes. The bad dream, the nightmare, was all round her. She tried to summon words, but she did not know where to start.

Nicolas stood over her, still as stone.

'You must have known that the time would come when you had to face me alone,' he said. 'Now it has come. We are here, you and I, and I am still waiting ...'

Carol moved her lips, but the words would not come. She made a great effort, and spoke slowly, trying to remember clearly in what order things had come about.

'The paper,' she said slowly, like a lesson repeated. 'I thought it was a warning. I thought that you—I was waiting for you to tell *me* why you had done it.'

'I!' the word exploded from Nicolas in a mixture of scorn and disbelief.

'I found the message in my glove,' Carol went on, carefully. 'I didn't know what to do. He was just like a real priest, and it was all in Latin. I tried to stop it all happening. But they thought I was acting. And you—you wouldn't let go. I tried . . . I tried to pull my hand away. But the ring . . .'

She looked down at her hand, where the ring shone red-gold in the light of the fading sun. 'And then—it was too late.'

Suddenly, it all seemed too much to bear. Tears, once they had begun, could not be held back. She found herself crying, silently, uncontrollably, too weak to make herself stop.

She could not see his face through the blur of tears, but for a moment she thought he made a movement towards her, and heard an exclamation of concern. But then he stiffened. His voice, when he spoke, was like ice.

'And what action,' he asked, 'had given you cause to think that I had marriage in mind?'

Carol turned her head away from the dark scorn in his eyes.

'Not only did I plan to marry you, it seems, but to force a marriage upon you.' The sarcasm in his voice cut like a dagger. 'And by stealth and deceit. Marriage—to a girl I had met only two days before. Is that the story you planned to tell the world? Your friends, your family, the press?'

His voice rose, drowning her cry of protest.

'But you will find that you have chosen the wrong man to play at marriage games. Was it blackmail? Did you hope to arrange a profitable annulment, perhaps, with your silence in return for my money?'

Carol made an effort to speak, but it was useless.

'Be quiet!' he said. 'I have no wish to listen to your lies. You were wrong when you said you could not act.' Every word was like a knife. 'I suppose it was not you who played the innocent that night, saying no, when you meant yes, saving yourself, bargaining with your body?'

'No. No, you're wrong—it wasn't. I didn't . . .' Carol said, desperately, but Nicolas took no notice, sweeping on like a storm which was nowhere near being spent.

'And it was not you who persuaded Varelle to ask me to take Anthony's place? You saw your chance—God knows how—and took it. Or was the good Kate in it with you? She could arrange anything—the perfect organiser! I suppose you will tell me that you were not discussing it with her that very afternoon. Oh, yes, my dear schemer—you did not know that I was near enough to overhear, not all, but enough to make it clear to me now the charming plot you were hatching between you.'

Carol could only gaze at him in horror. Her voice would not come. She knew now—she had time to think—what it meant to be struck dumb. In any case, Nicolas was in no mood to listen.

'And then,' he went on, the contempt in his voice cutting across her thoughts, 'what exquisite shyness when you tried to drag away your hand! Such a reluctant bride, fighting for her freedom, but at the last giving in to what you had planned all the time. And now these tears, these so very convincing signs of weakness ... If I had not seen through your game, my fair gambler, they might have seemed real even to me. But no, Calypso, you were indeed wrong. You *can* act. As an actress you could have a most impressive career.'

As one accusation followed another, Carol tried to protest, to deny each monstrous misinterpretation of what had happened. But it was impossible, as impossible as it would have been to stop the angry waves from breaking on the shore, or to switch off a flash of lightning. Her head was bursting, and she pressed her hands to her forehead in an effort to think. It might even be that Nicolas was putting on a performance himself, to confuse her, to mask the truth. If this were so, there was nothing she could say which would be of the slightest use.

Carol had shut her eyes, to shut out his anger, to hold it away from her, as if by so doing she could avoid the hurt he was causing with every word. The whole thing was a nightmare. It was worse than a nightmare. At least with a bad dream, you woke up. You opened your eyes very wide, and the worst of dreams faded away, leaving you thankful and alone.

She opened her eyes, but the dream did not fade. Nicolas

was still there. He had turned half away from her, and was pouring wine into a glass. He held it out to her.

'Drink this,' he ordered, his voice now calm and controlled. 'You will need it. So much planning, such acting, they do you credit. But sometimes even the best plans go wrong, my Calypso. And this time, you will find that you have achieved rather more than you intended. Drink.'

Carol obeyed him.

'There will be no blackmail. No scandal. No payment in return for hushing up what would make me the laughing stock of my country. No convenient annulment. You have begun something which will be finished in *my* way, not yours. You wanted a marriage. Then, my dear, you shall have one. But it will be rather more real than you had schemed for.'

'I don't understand you,' Carol said. She tried to pull her thoughts together, but the wine made it even more difficult than before. 'I don't know what you mean. All I know is that I'm going home tomorrow, whatever happens, whatever has happened already. I can't stay here. You must see that.'

'It's not quite so easy, my dear Calypso. Have you forgotten so soon that you are my wife?'

He laughed, and the sound was so bitter, so harsh, that Carol covered her eyes with her hand.

She did not see him leave the room. It was the bang of the door, and the sound of his footsteps striding away, which told her that she was alone, if only for a moment. She did not waste time trying to make out what he had meant. Her only thought was to escape, and quickly, to escape from the house, from his anger, from whatever it was he planned to do.

Getting up from the day bed brought on a wave of dizziness, and, although she had kicked off her slippers, the clothes she was wearing made any kind of haste difficult. She wished she could take them off, too, but dared not spend precious minutes fumbling with the many fastenings. The stiff brocade skirts were not only heavy, but made a swishing sound which Carol was sure could be heard all over the house. She held them close to her, and away from the floor, as she tiptoed across the room to the door.

Hardly daring to breathe, she opened it and crossed the courtyard to the delicate iron gates which led to the long drive. The ironwork was wrought into the shape of two graceful peacocks, back to back; there was no padlock that she could see, and she pushed them gently open, hoping that no creak or clang would betray her.

Then she was away. Her bare feet made no sound as she slipped down the long straight drive between the crumbling walls, half running, half walking, as fast as the cumbersome dress would allow.

When she was well out of earshot, she began to wish that she had brought the shoes with her. The loose stones of the drive cut her feet, and when she tried to walk on the narrow verge she discovered that it was covered with a kind of thistle whose spiny thorns were more painful than any stone.

The dusk was rapidly turning to darkness, and Carol was not afraid that Nicolas would see her from the house. But she would not feel at all safe until she was out on the road. Almost half a mile away, at the end of the drive, stood the two great gateposts. She could see them as she ran, but it seemed as if she would never reach them. If only she could get to them before Nicolas realised she was gone . . . Elaine's words flashed back into her mind: 'He hunts women as other men hunt game.' They had a more sinister meaning now. He would hunt her down, take pleasure in pursuing her . . .

But, once on the road, surely she could find her way to safety? She had only the vaguest memory of where the *palazzo* was in relation to the film company's encampment, but she had no doubt that any passing car would give her a lift, probably take her straight there. And once she was surrounded by the film people, even Nicolas could hardly drag her away, caveman-fashion. And perhaps Carlos's substitute would have been found, and would turn out not to have been a priest after all, and the whole nightmarish affair could come to an end.

After what seemed an age, the gateposts had stopped being small and far away, and loomed large and shadowy at either side. With immense relief, and renewed confidence, Carol stepped out on to the smoother surface of the road.

She hoped that she did not look too strange a sight for anyone to stop for. A sixteenth-century wedding dress was not an ideal garment for running away in, but most of the Gozitans would know about the film, she reminded herself, and their natural good manners would not question, she hoped, why she should be hurrying along a country road alone, with no shoes.

At last the sound of a car behind her made her turn, and hold up her hand to face the oncoming headlights, headlights which spelt freedom and people and friends and home. Dazzled by the glare, she wondered if the car would pass her, leaving her stranded and alone once more, but then they dimmed, the noise of the engine changed, and the car slowed to a halt beside her.

Too late, she recognised the scarlet sports car. Nicolas leaned across to open the door on the passenger side.

'Get in,' he said shortly.

'Will you take me home?' Carol faced him, standing her ground, trying to tell herself that she was not afraid of him, no matter what his reputation might be, that he could do her no real harm, after all.

'Just get in,' he repeated. 'Unless you want me to bundle your skirts over your head and shut you in the boot, in the manner of a true kidnapper. It would be less trouble, but uncivilised, and not very dignified for either of us.'

Carol hesitated. If she ran, or tried to run in her long heavy skirts, Carol had no doubt that Nicolas would catch her up in seconds, and that he would certainly do what he threatened.

'I think I have told you before,' he added, 'that I am stronger than you. Unfair, but an indisputable fact.'

So it was that once more she found herself sitting beside him in his car. And once more he drove at a breathtaking pace, but this time in a silence heavy with unspoken purpose on his part, barely stifled fear on hers.

They twisted and turned along roads Carol did not recognise in the dusk. It must have been on the wilder side of the island, for they passed no towns, and came to no landmark which she could identify. The high hedges of grey-green prickly pear had given way to fields with walls of stone, and Carol guessed that the sea was not far away. She thought she saw the gleam of water, once, and heard the sound of waves breaking against rocks.

It seemed to Carol like an hour, but it could not have been much more than fifteen or twenty minutes before the car began to climb steeply.

'Where are you taking me?' Carol asked, in a voice which she tried to keep steady.

Nicolas stared straight ahead. 'You will see,' was all he would say.

Remembering the formidable cliffs with their sheer drop of over four hundred feet, Carol spent some uneasy moments wondering if Nicolas planned to solve his difficulties by murder. 'She stood too near the edge,' he could say. 'I tried to warn her, but she wouldn't listen.' How easy it would be, with no one to see him push her over the edge, no one to hear her scream before she hit the rocks below.

When he stopped the car and Carol looked about her, she thought she had never seen a more lonely place. They had come along one of the narrow side tracks which led from the road to a headland of rocky scrub. In silhouette against the sea and sky was the square block shape of a tower, one of the towers built hundreds of years before to defend the island from the Turkish marauders from the sea. Nicolas had pointed them out to her before. They stood in isolated, commanding positions, overlooking the approach routes of the enemy vessels, solid and strong to withstand assault.

But why had Nicolas brought her here?

Carol had no time to speculate. As soon as he had helped, or rather pulled, Carol from the passenger seat, he was guiding her with a firm hand on her arm towards the tower.

She tried to hang back, to stand her ground, but Nicolas was too strong for her to resist.

'Where are we?' she said. 'Why have you brought me here?'

'It's not a palace,' Nicolas said, not relaxing his hold. 'But it will do very well for the present. You will find that it is a little more comfortable than when it was built. And from the top you will have a splendid view.'

'Surely,' said Carol, trying to play for time, 'you haven't brought me here to show me the view?'

'How very observant of you,' he said drily. 'I commend your reasoning powers. No. It has other advantages. Privacy is one. And security.'

'You're not proposing that I should stay here?' said Carol, realising that that was probably what he did intend.

'I think you will find it convenient,' he said, as they passed under a massive archway. 'For the moment, until I have decided what is the best way of managing our affairs.'

The floor of the tower was of bare earth, pressed as hard as stone. The surrounding walls were massive, dark, and chill, and Nicolas guided Carol to one corner, where a flight of stone steps inside the wall led up to the floor above.

Nicolas pressed a switch and a lamp shone from the wall, down on to the ancient steps, their treads worn to a curve in the middle.

'Easy to defend,' Nicolas said, conversationally, as if he were a kindly host instead of—what? A gaoler about to shut her up in a medieval prison? A kidnapper? Although she was trembling with fatigue, Carol summoned the strength to climb the stone steps. They led up to a door of blackened wood, with a great iron handle.

'The key is quite modern,' said Nicolas. 'Disappointing but none the less effective.' With the hand which was not grasping Carol's arm he unlocked the door, which swung inwards, easily and silently.

'Go in,' Nicolas ordered, and Carol, having no option, obeyed. In doing so, she crossed what seemed like a time threshold, straight from the sixteenth to the twentieth century.

There were creamy rugs on a polished wood floor, a glass lamp like a moon on a table of pale marble; but she had time only to register these, to notice the shuttered windows and two further doors; then she heard the sound of a key turning, and looked back to find that the door had closed and she was alone.

Furiously she beat on the door with her fists, but it was as hard and as solid as iron. She ran to the window, wrenched open one of the shutters and leaned out. Her heart missed a beat. It was as Nicolas had said. The tower must be perched on the edge of the cliff. Far, far below her, at the bottom of a sheer wall of cliff, were rocks, and the sea.

On the other side of the room there was a deep embrasure, sloping in from a wide opening to a mere slit. Realising that this was one of the arrow-slit openings she had seen from the ground, Carol ran over to it, and was just in time to see the headlights of Nicolas's car as he drove away.

Without much hope, she went back to the door and examined it. The handle on her side was of a pale blue-green polished stone, and below it was a keyhole. It must be meant to be opened from the inside as well as from the other. The room did not look like a prison cell, more like a luxury flat. If this was so, there was just a chance that she might find a duplicate key, in one of the drawers of the desk, perhaps; though Nicolas was not the kind of man to have overlooked such a thing.

During the search which followed, Carol discovered that she was imprisoned not in one room, but in a suite of four. One door opened into a bedroom, with its own bathroom, the other into a small but well-designed kitchen. It looked almost unused. The drawers in the fitted cupboards were as tidy as if they had never been pulled out before. Those in the dressing-table were empty. Beyond the kitchen there was a smaller bedroom, and that was as bare as a monk's cell.

Carol came back to the large room with its moon lamp, the white armchairs, marble-topped table, and the wide desk, which took up the whole space in front of one of the shuttered windows. Beside it was a cabinet with shallow drawers, but all she could find in them were plans and papers, engineers' drawings, sheets of figures, and maps. The drawers in the desk were locked.

Defeated, Carol sat down in one of the armchairs, and tried to think calmly about the predicament she was in. There was no need to despair, she told herself. The time would have to come when the film people missed her. Kate would be wondering where she was already, and why she had not come back to finish her packing. Besides, Kate knew that Nicolas had taken her away in his car, saying that he would look after her. That might mean that she would not start worrying until the next day, when the film company was due to leave. There was to be a party tonight, but Kate would only think that she had not felt well enough to come.

Carol felt her spirits drop. There would be no search parties going out for her until the following day. Then she remembered the pay that was due to her, and her hopes revived. She had not yet collected her money for the three days of film work, and Kate would know that; she knew everything. She might begin to worry when Carol did not come back for her things, but she would be certain that something was wrong if Carol's pay was unclaimed.

So what would they do, when she did not return to the film camp? They would ask Nicolas, and Nicolas, however unscrupulous a liar, would not be able to give a plausible reason for her total disappearance. Kate would make a fuss. Varelle would lose his temper. Nicolas would have to let her go. He couldn't really mean to keep her here, against her will, locked up, a prisoner. It was unthinkable.

Exhausted with worry, Carol let her head fall back against the chair and shut her eyes.

She woke to the sound of someone moving about in the kitchen. There was a sound as of a saucepan being put down, and then the chink of a spoon in a glass. Whoever it was had come softly, quietly, for Carol had not woken, had heard nothing. Was it Nicolas? And if so, what could she say to persuade him to let her go?

'Who's there?' she called. Before she could pull herself up from the deep chair, a dark, bent figure had flitted like a shadow from the kitchen, and Carol recognised the old lace-maker, Ta Dentella, who had nursed Nicolas as a child. She stood before Carol now, a calm smile on her old face, and a glass of something in her hand.

'It is milk, *madame*,' she said. 'Very nice for you. Drink it. I have made it warm for you, with honey in it also. You will feel much more better.'

As she obediently drank the comforting warm milk, Carol wondered if it was her reassuring smile or her calm, unhurried manner which had been the secret of Ta

Dentella's success in the nursery.

'You are tired, so tired,' she said, watching Carol drink. 'And I do not want to wake you. But when you have drunk this milk. I will help you to undress, and you shall have a bath, which I prepare for you. And then I cook you a nice, nice supper, and you will feel more better, much more better.'

'But . . .' Carol began.

'But now you do not talk. Come. I take the glass, and now I help you with your dress. It is so beautiful. It becomes you very well, to be a bride.'

Talking all the time, and fluttering round Carol like a black moth, the old woman unfastened the ties and laces and hooks of the heavy costume. But her soothing murmur, though it calmed Carol's fears, explained nothing.

To all Carol's questions—had the Baron brought her? Was he coming back? Why was he keeping her, Carol, here?—she shook her head and spoke words as soft as caresses, leaving more than half unanswered.

Yes, the Baron always knew what was best to do. No, Carol was not to worry about anything. No harm could come to her, she might be sure, while the Baron's orders were obeyed.

Clearly, in the eyes of his old nurse, Nicolas could do no wrong, and Carol soon gave up trying to find out anything from Ta Dentella. Obediently she stepped out of the heavy brocade folds of the dress, allowed herself to be wrapped in a white silk robe and pushed gently towards the bathroom, where she stepped into a milky-green bath smelling of rosemary.

The supper which Ta Dentella cooked for her was as delicious as she had promised, and so light and easy to eat that Carol suspected it might have been one of Nicolas's favourites as a child. There were eggs in it, and tomatoes, herbs, and the finest of pasta, thinner than the thinnest vermicelli. Ta Dentella took away her plate, smiling to see that it was empty, and said, 'Now it is time for bed, my child.'

Carol did not protest. She was so drowsy that she wondered if there had been something in the milk, or the food, or whether it was all the emotion and excitement of that extraordinary day.

Events had happened so fast one upon another that now Carol thought of them as happening a long way away, a long time ago, almost to another person. It no longer seemed worth the effort of wondering if she could possibly be Nicolas's wife, as well as his prisoner, or what would happen to her tomorrow.

Nothing seemed to matter any more. There was something so soothing in the soft light by the bed, and the gentle sounds made by the old woman in the other room, that before she knew it Carol was asleep.

CHAPTER SIX

WITH the morning came memory, sharp and worrying; breakfast, in the sun, facing the sea; and a long period of planning what she would say to Nicolas when he came. For surely he must come, at best to release her, at the worst to explain what he meant to do with her.

Ta Dentella busied herself with household chores, refusing to speak at all.

'There is a time for talking,' she said, with a touch of severity, 'and a time for work,' and left Carol free to think over all the arguments and pleas and persuasions she could possibly use to bring Nicolas to his senses, when he came. For come he must; of that Carol was sure. And by this time, all the muddle would surely have been cleared up—or so said half her mind. He would have seen Kate. He would have discovered the name of the actor. He would have to come back to let her out, to apologise—though an apology might be too much to ask.

The other half continued to torment her with doubts and fears about Nicolas, his motives, his supposed hatred of women, his contempt for herself, his anger, his pride. Even if he were wrong, how could a man like Nicolas bring himself to admit it?

When he did come, it was nearly noon, and Carol soon realised that she might as well have saved herself the trouble of worrying about anything she might have to say to him.

It was a stiff and formal visit, more like a consultation

with a solicitor, she thought. She had been disconcerted to find her heart going like a hammer when Ta Dentella announced his arrival.

'I'm surprised that you found it necessary to knock,' she said, ungraciously. 'I thought that as a gaoler you could come and go exactly as you pleased.'

Nicolas's dark eyes met hers with controlled calm.

'I am not your gaoler,' he said. 'The door is not locked; there is nothing to prevent you from opening it.'

'Nothing to—— Oh, no! You mean, last night, I could have walked out? Any time?'

'Once I had installed your chaperon,' he said.

'So I could go now?' said Carol.

'To walk about the countryside in nothing but a white silk wrap would not be a good idea,' Nicolas answered, looking her up and down slowly and dispassionately. 'I might think it wise to stop you from making a fool of yourself.'

'By what right?' Carol demanded, as furious as he was calm.

'A husband,' said Nicolas evenly, 'has certain marital rights. And one is to make sure that his wife does not drag his name—I believe the expression is—in the dust.'

'Husband,' said Carol, her face pale. She had been so buoyed up by the subconscious hope that the mystery of the priest who was not an actor—or the actor who was not a priest—would have been straightened out, that his words were like a dash of cold water.

'Did you find the priest?' she asked. 'Is it true that he *is* one?'

'He took his pay and went,' said Nicolas. 'As you must have known, once he disappeared from the island I should have to go to the police if I wanted to trace him. And this you knew quite well I would never do.'

'Why?' said Carol. 'We *must* find him.'

'It does you credit,' said Nicolas with an ironic bow, 'to appear so anxious for him to be found. But it will not do, my dear. As it is impossible for me to search for him, I have had to give him the benefit of the doubt.'

'And?'

'And assume that he was.' Carol drew a deep breath. 'In which case,' Nicolas continued, as coolly as if he were chairing a business meeting, 'we are married, you and I.'

Carol shut her eyes, and leaned back in her chair.

'Yes,' he went on. 'It is an intolerable situation. There was no certificate, no entry in the register. There were witnesses, it is true, but they were all strangers. Most shameful, most—laughable—of all, the marriage took place entirely without the knowledge, or the participation, of my family. The disgrace——' he paused '—the disgrace would be something which you could not be expected to understand.'

Carol sat up, stung by the scorn in that cold voice.

'How could I?' she said hotly. '*I* am only a blackmailer. It is of course no shame or disgrace for *me*—to have been kidnapped, married against my will to a tyrannical madman, accused of being a schemer and a liar, and then shut up in a tower like something out of Grimms' Fairy Stories!'

'Lower your voice,' he said, 'or Ta Dentella may think that you are angry with me. And that would upset her quite surprisingly.'

'I wonder how she could possibly be so mistaken,' Carol said. She smiled sweetly at Nicolas as the old woman carried in a silver tray with two long glasses of iced coffee and a plate of small biscuits, thin as a wafer and tasting of almonds.

'Ta Dentella will never believe a word said against me—is that not so?' he asked his old nurse.

'The perfect chaperon, in fact,' Carol murmured, as Ta Dentella smiled, and nodded, and melted away to her kitchen.

'Ta Dentella is looking after you well, I hope?' Nicolas asked, with formal politeness.

'As a prison wardress,' said Carol, 'she is probably the most gentle ever invented. But aren't you afraid that I shall knock her on the head, steal her clothes and escape?'

Nicolas gazed at her thoughtfully. 'No,' he said, his eyes unwavering. 'No, I am not afraid of that. What good would it do you to escape? Would you go home to your friends and explain to them that you contrived to marry a man for purposes of blackmail, and were now returning to the fold, still married to him, and without the money?'

Carol gave a deep sigh, and twisted the wedding ring on her finger round and round.

'Look,' she said. 'Is it any use me telling you that I did *not* contrive anything of the kind? That it is all as much a mystery to me as you say it is to you, and was probably some stupid practical joke of Elaine's—or someone . . .' Her voice trailed off.

Nicolas looked dispassionately at her. 'No use at all,' he said. 'I have already told you, I have called your bluff, and you must take the consequences. How it happened is no longer relevant. The fact is that it has. And there is only one way to put it right. I think you will agree, when I give you the outlines of the plan I have in mind, that it is the only sensible solution.'

Almost, Carol wished that he would be angry, would

shout at her, lose his temper. That would have been easier to deal with, less frightening than this deadly coolness.

'What do you propose?' she asked.

'A wedding.' The answer was devastatingly unexpected. 'But this time in public, with everything done as it should be done.'

'You *are* mad,' Carol said, but she might have been talking to a block of granite.

'First,' he said, disregarding her efforts to interrupt him, 'you will meet my family. I shall already have told them the glad news of our betrothal. They will offer you their congratulations to cover their surprise.'

'Will you tell them how we met—how you swept me off my feet?' Carol asked, but Nicolas took no notice. Only a flicker at the corner of his mouth showed that he remembered very well.

'I shall tell them that we met during the making of the film—I knew there was a curse on this film—that there was a whirlwind courtship, very romantic for both of us, and that we are to be married without delay.'

'Won't that seem very sudden?'

'My impatience is a legend at Xatahn—a byword,' he said with a sardonic smile. 'They know that I cannot wait to take possession of such a desirable piece of property. Your dowry—or lack of it—will shock them very much more than the shortness of our engagement.'

'How short, exactly?' asked Carol, wondering how he could be so calm, so sure that she would fall in with his preposterous plan.

'By custom the marriage has to take place in the parish of the bride,' he went on, 'which is why I chose Torri ta Xiri for your residence during the qualifying three weeks. It is in the same parish as Xatahn.'

'On your land,' murmured Carol. 'One of your goods and chattels.'

'It will be in the chapel one of my ancestors had built for his particular patron saint; it is not far from the Palazzo ta Xatahn.' He reached out to take one of the tall glasses of iced coffee. It was quite extraordinary, Carol thought, to be sitting so quietly, so composedly, as if they were discussing not their wedding, but the weather, or the harvest, or the market price of melons.

'And what about my family?' Carol asked, thinking that John would find it hard to believe any of the recent events. She could not imagine him even beginning to take them seriously.

'I seem to remember that—conveniently—you have no parents to be unduly shocked or alarmed by your inexplicable alliance with a stranger,' he said, thoughtfully stirring the melting ice in his glass with a long spoon. 'But your brother—John?—will no doubt wish to represent your family at the marriage ceremony.'

'You have thought of everything,' Carol said, wishing she could sting him out of his infuriating composure. 'Perhaps because it is not altogether a new experience for you, getting married. Or preparing for it.'

For one unguarded instant, his eyes blazed, and the hand which held the glass so negligently shook. But the anger was controlled almost before it had shown itself.

'Your brother,' he continued, as if she had not spoken. 'We were talking of your brother. I have already sent a cable to him, informing him, on your behalf, of the joyful news.'

'John?' Carol was startled. 'How could you have done that? You don't have his address.'

'It is on one of your cases,' said Nicolas. 'Did you borrow

one of his? Oh, they are outside. I fetched them last night.'

'You've seen the film people?' said Carol.

'Of course. I told Kate that you were sorry to miss the farewell party, but you did not feel well enough to go. She quite understood.'

'What else did you tell them?' Carol asked, her heart sinking. She had counted on Kate, at least, being worried about her non-appearance.

'That I and my people would look after you until you were fit to travel. Also that I would take charge of your pay packet.'

'Very clever,' said Carol. 'How kind of you. How thoughtful.'

'Kate sent her love, by the way,' he went on, choosing to ignore the interruption. 'She was sorry to hear that you were not strong enough even for a visit, or she would have been sure to come to say goodbye. As for Elaine . . .' He paused, and his face hardened.

'Yes? Did she send her love, too?' Carol tried to keep her voice light. He must not see how scared she was beginning to feel.

'All she passed on was your extremely illuminating conversation with her before you laid your little trap.'

'What conversation?' Carol asked, genuinely puzzled.

'You were very anxious to know, apparently, whether the chapel was still consecrated. You even joked about the fact that a real priest was all that was needed to turn the film marriage into a legal one.'

'But that's all it was,' Carol protested. 'A joke. And *I* didn't ask her . . .' She tried to remember those idle words of hers—or had it been Kate's? 'At least, I don't think . . .' She stopped, unable to go on. What was the use, when Nicolas so obviously thought she was lying?

She clutched at one last straw.

'What's to stop me walking out of here and finding the film people and telling them that you've kidnapped me?'

'Several things,' said Nicolas impassively. He looked at his watch. 'One, they are not on Gozo. They left this morning. Two, I do not think you would go very far with no money. You might sell your camera for a few pounds, perhaps, but I would not advise it. I do not think that a woman of your independent spirit would like to be fetched back to Xatahn like a runaway child.'

'No money?' said Carol. 'But you said ...'

'I said I would be happy to take care of it for you,' Nicolas said, the smoothness of his voice masking the iron-hard face. 'Even if you had money for the ferry, you would get no further than the airport in Malta.'

'What do you mean?' Carol asked, and Nicolas answered her with bland unconcern for her rising anger.

'You would find it difficult to board an aircraft without a passport,' he said.

Carol lost her temper. 'You took my passport?' she said. 'I insist, I *demand* that you give it back. And stop acting as if you were a medieval overlord,' she added, annoyed to find that she had a childish desire to scream and stamp her foot.

His eyebrows lifted, and a half smile made his face look more like a devilish mask than ever.

'You will not want an out-of-date passport,' he said.

'It's not out of date!' Carol exclaimed. 'I had it two years ago.'

'Not officially out of date,' he agreed, 'but I am sure you will have no use for one with your old name on it. I shall give you the forms to sign with your new signature as soon as they arrive.'

So that was that. Game, set and match to Nicolas. Carol

fought down a desire to hit out at the man sitting opposite her and watching her with a certain amused detachment, as if he could read the angry thoughts inside her head.

'What else have you arranged?' she asked, instead. 'An announcement in *The Times*?'

'The announcements have already been sent to the English papers,' Nicolas told her. 'They will come out tomorrow, or Thursday at the latest.'

'You seem to have thought of everything,' Carol said. 'All very cut and dried. Do I have any say in the matter, or are you taking my agreement for granted?'

'There is nothing for you to agree to,' Nicolas said, standing up as if his business were done.

'Just sign on the dotted line when the time comes,' said Carol, staring at him. How could he be so insufferably calm? 'Tell me one thing. Have you always had your own way? All your life?'

'It is usually the best way,' said Nicolas with no trace of boasting in his voice, as if he were stating an obvious fact. 'And now . . .' He made a move towards the door, but Carol stood and faced him, pulling the white silk wrap close about her like a cloak of dignity.

'One thing more,' she said. 'I don't understand how you can want to tie yourself to me at all. If I am what you think I am, why do you want to be married to such a lying, scheming, crooked creature?'

He looked at her coldly. 'Most women fit that description,' he said. 'And you are the latest to teach me that they can never be trusted, no matter how charming. It is in their nature, ever since Eve, to be crooked. Not a pleasant word, crooked. Devious is perhaps better. And I dare say you are no more devious than any other.'

Carol could find no words to deny this monstrous, sweeping charge.

'Besides,' he said, his hand on the door, 'the idea of being married to you is beginning to amuse me. Married on my terms, not yours,' he added. He bent to kiss her hand, and did not release it when he straightened. For a moment they stood face to face, so close as to be almost touching, and Carol thought that Nicolas was about to take her in his arms as he had done on the hill above Ramla. There was something in his eyes that she could not fathom, but then he laughed, and stepped back, letting her go.

'You need not worry,' he said. 'I may be your husband, you may already be my legal wife. But I have no intention, yet, of consummating our somewhat irregular marriage. I can wait, and three weeks is not a long time.'

Three weeks, Carol thought when he had gone, and her anger and fear had subsided a little—she had three weeks. Surely that would be long enough to sort out the mess she was in: to get away, to try to find out the truth, to shake herself free from a man who did not love her, and who wanted her only to satisfy his own overbearing feelings of power and pride.

She would have to wait for the right moment. Whatever she did, she must be absolutely sure of success before she made her move. Nicolas had told her that she was not a prisoner in the tower, but Carol could not bear to think of the fuss and disgrace which would follow an unsuccessful attempt at escape. For a day or two at least she would appear to fall in with his plans, and act the part of loving fiancée.

It was on the very next day that Nicolas presented her, formally, and with every evidence of restrained affection, to his mother. Carol had expected this meeting to be an ordeal, and so it was, but of a very different kind from anything she had imagined. She had prepared herself to meet a dragon, and a none-too-friendly dragon at that. She had not expected to be welcomed with affection and delight.

'So you are the remarkable one who is to make my son happy,' said the Baroness, taking Carol's hand and looking straight into her eyes. She had the same eyes as Nicolas— very dark, very direct—and when she smiled, it was his smile, but without the irony or the cynicism which had painted harsh lines on her son's face. With her coil of white hair encircling her head like a crown, she looked more like a queen than a dragon.

'You have taken on a task which I hope will give you— both of you—much joy,' she said, 'but which may have its times of storm and tempest.' She smiled at Nicolas, and turned to Carol again. 'You must not let Nicolas bully you. He has been the Baron of Xatahn for so many years that he is a little in danger of becoming a tyrant.'

In danger of? thought Carol, but she was too bewildered at being greeted so kindly to do little more than blush, and stammer something about doing her best. Knowing that Nicolas's sardonic gaze was on her made her nervous, and she was relieved when the Baroness sent him to the study.

'There are papers I know you want to see; they are on the desk.'

'How *you* can speak of tyrants . . .' said Nicolas, laughing at her, but he went, leaving the two women alone together.

'Come and sit in the garden,' the Baroness said, 'while it is still cool enough to enjoy the air outside, and you shall tell me everything.'

If only she could, Carol thought, as she followed her through the tall unshuttered windows on to a stone terrace, with steps which led down into what looked like a valley of flowering trees and shrubs.

'You like it?' the Baroness asked, when Carol gave an exclamation of pleasure. 'It is a little like the artificial valley in the San Anton Gardens. Did you see very much of Malta before you came over here?'

She did not ask about Nicolas, or how they had met, and Carol was thankful to be spared the task of having to skirt the truth.

'Why did you not warn me about your mother?' Carol asked Nicolas when he drove her back to the tower.

'Was there a need to warn you? Was she so very formidable?'

'Not formidable,' said Carol. 'Enchanting. So—so welcoming. It makes me feel such a fraud.'

Nicolas turned his head to look at her, then gave his attention to the road.

'That seems only just,' he said, flatly.

'How can you do this to her?' Carol asked.

'Do what?'

'You know what I mean—your whole plan. It's so false.'

'What do you think it would do to her,' said Nicolas grimly, 'to learn the truth? That her son was tricked into marriage in a way which could have brought the name of our family on to the front page of the gutter press? That the Baron of Xatahn had been made a laughing stock, a dupe, the prey of a blackmailer and an extortionist?'

Carol pressed her lips tightly together. She, too, could be proud. What use was it to go on pleading her innocence, when he was so determined not to believe her?

'It is to cause my mother the smallest possible distress,' he went on, 'that I am carrying this matter to its only proper conclusion. It does not worry me in the least that you feel a fraud. I am not concerned with your finer feelings, my dear bride, but with the good name, the honour, and the feelings of my family. And don't underrate your powers of deception. You should be able to fool my aunts and cousins and uncles quite easily, as you almost succeeded in fooling me.'

At the betrothal party, which the Baroness held for Carol to meet the rest of the family, she soon saw that they needed no convincing. They were all only too ready to believe that Carol and Nicolas were happily and properly in love.

Carol wore a dress made from one of her own fabrics, a swirl of blues and greens which brought out the colour in her eyes. As she and Nicolas circled the two great salons, shaking hands with the first cousins, second cousins, uncles, aunts and other more distant relations, there were murmurs of admiration as well as congratulations.

'My dear,' said the most outspoken of the aunts. 'I can see why Nicolas is *épris*. You are quite lovely. It must have been breathtakingly romantic.' She was thin, vital and dark, and dressed in colours which made her look like some vivid tropical bird. 'And did you really meet only such a short while ago?' Hardly pausing for an answer, she went on. 'How it reminds me . . . Oh, never mind, it is better not to think of the past. These whirlwind romances were not the thing in the old days, you know. Everything had to be arranged with such formality. Meetings between both sets of parents. Then the lengthy discussions about settlements, and so on.'

'Carol's parents are both dead,' Nicolas said quickly, 'so that custom, alas, cannot be followed.'

'I am so sorry. I am a tactless creature. But even if they had been still living, it would not have been easy for you, my dearest Nicolas, to have called upon them. So far away.

England is a good deal further than Malta, for instance.'

'It is indeed,' Carol said, taking a sidelong look at Nicolas's inscrutable face. 'Sometimes it seems as far off as the moon.'

'But then everything is so different nowadays,' the aunt rattled on. 'I remember even the last time, Nicolas, that you . . .'

'Aunt Lucia, you must tell Carol about your passionate interest in the crafts of Gozo,' said Nicolas, interrupting the flow of words. Carol wondered if his birdlike aunt had been about to launch into an indiscreet comparison between his forthcoming marriage arrangements and those of the past.

She could never ask him. For now, and during the days which followed, Nicolas was two different people.

At the betrothal party and during the round of visits afterwards, he played the part of an attentive escort. Guiding her from one group of relations to another, or introducing her to yet another elderly cousin, he did not refer openly to his supposed love for Carol. Instead, he let it be seen, by the way his eyes rested on her, and the smile which still had the power to make her heart turn over, that he considered himself to be what one jovial uncle called 'the luckiest man in Gozo'.

But as soon as they were alone, driving back to the tower, all signs of affection vanished. The coolness returned, the sardonic manner, and a certain amused contempt which Carol found hard to bear. Although he had said that he was not her gaoler, it seemed to Carol that he derived much enjoyment from putting a stop to any chance of escape which came her way.

There was the time when Aunt Lucia invited her to stay with her. 'It is too bad that Nicolas keeps you hidden away in that old fortress,' she declared. 'You shall come to me, and we shall really enjoy ourselves!'

But Nicolas simply laughed and shook his head, saying that he knew better than to entrust Carol to her care.

'You have too many protegées already on Gozo. You would wear her out by dragging her from one workshop to another, and, besides, you would talk the poor girl's head off her shoulders. No, my dearest Aunt, Carol is best where she is.' His tone was light and bantering, but Carol could hear the steel beneath.

'Then at least I insist on helping her to choose the trousseau,' Aunt Lucia said. 'You will need evening dresses, and there will be the lingerie. Nicolas, dear boy, make yourself scarce. There is a woman who makes wonderful embroidered silk nightdresses; I shall bring her to you myself tomorrow. And the shoemaker—Paul is best——'

'But I could drive in to Victoria to see the dressmaker,' said Carol. If she and Aunt Lucia went shopping together, she thought, it would be a simple matter to slip away and catch a bus to Mgarr, and get away on the ferry. She glanced at her engagement ring; perhaps she could sell it. It was a diamond, set between two sapphires—'To match your eyes,' Nicolas had murmured, and only Carol had known that he was mocking her.

Aunt Lucia opened her mouth to answer, but Nicolas interrupted smoothly and swiftly, as if he had read Carol's thoughts.

'It is more fitting,' he said, 'that they should come here to you.'

'He is wrong, of course,' said Aunt Lucia, 'but the poor boy must be humoured.'

'I am glad you think so,' said Nicolas gravely.

'That is something you cannot learn too early, my dear child,' Aunt Lucia went on, 'that humouring a man is the very essence of a happy marriage.'

'I thought only dangerous madmen needed humouring,' said Carol, looking very hard at Nicolas, but he only smiled at her with apparent charm.

'Aunt Lucia will tell you that in her opinion all men must be humoured for that very reason,' he said.

'Not all men,' Aunt Lucia contradicted him. 'Not all are mad—only those who are in love. Then they are insane beyond curing!' And she shook her head at her nephew.

Nicolas laughed, and his eyes met Carol's, but she turned away. She was not sure that she could keep up this game of make-believe which came so easily to him.

For all the preparations of the wedding, the coming and going of dressmaker, hairdresser, shoemaker and others involved in making Carol a bride fit for their Baron, were like some strange and hectic charade, a pageant in which all the cast were real, except for herself and Nicolas.

They were the only actors: Nicolas, playing the part of an attentive bridegroom almost as if he enjoyed it, and herself, waiting, waiting for a chance to step off the stage on which she found herself an unwilling performer and run, and run, back to her own real world again.

But it was not so easy to step off that stage, she found. She could not leave the tower unless Nicolas fetched her; it was too far away and too exposed for her to be able to walk along the winding road without being seen. At night, when he brought her back from an evening engagement, he handed her in to a warm welcome from Ta Dentella.

The old lace-maker loved nothing better than to fuss round Carol and promise Nicolas that she would lock up everything safely. 'For you are his precious jewel,' she told Carol. 'Who else should look after such a jewel but Ta Dentella?'

What was it Rosie had said, in that last evening of carefree chatter? Something about the wicked Baron bearing her away to his castle keep, Carol remembered. Those words, spoken so light-heartedly, had come only too true. Whatever would Rosie say if she knew?

Then it came to her. She could not escape on her own; she had to have help from outside. If she wrote a letter to Rosie—John was away, she knew—perhaps she could find a way to have it posted without Nicolas finding out.

Late at night, when Ta Dentella thought her asleep, Carol wrote her letter. It was a long one, and in it Carol poured out all that had happened, how the announcements in the English newspapers had been put in without her knowledge or consent, and how the wedding was taking place only because of a terrible accident which she could not yet explain, and might never be able to explain while she was a virtual prisoner, unable to find out the truth. She begged Rosie to contact John and make him come over to take her away.

'He's the head of the family,' she wrote, 'and here that really counts. I don't care what he says or does, as long as he stops the marriage.'

The dawn was breaking as she re-read the hastily written pages—and there were many of them, besides the ones torn up on the floor—and stuffed them into an envelope. Her big problem now was how to post it, and on reflection she thought she might make an unwitting ally of Aunt Lucia.

'Will you post a letter for me?' Carol asked as she said goodbye after a morning of fittings. 'It's to a friend in London. I don't want Nicolas to know.'

Aunt Lucia's eyebrows shot up, and her mouth was pursed.

'Is it to a man? But of course not—unless it is to tell him

you are engaged and to give him his *congé* . . .'

'No, no! Aunt Lucia, look at the address. It's to a friend. I want her to buy a very special present, for Nicolas. She knows the shop.'

'Ah, a secret! But how romantic. Have you a stamp? No matter, I can see to that. What are you giving him?'

As Carol could not think of anything on the spur of the moment, she laughed and said that Aunt Lucia would have to wait and see.

Carol saw her push the letter into the back flap of her handbag, and began to count the days before help would come. It would take two days, say, to reach Rosie. Then Rosie would have to find John and convince him that Carol needed him urgently. He would be furious; it would totally disorganise his routine, and interrupt the conference which she knew was an important one. But she knew that he would come.

Solid, dependable John—a surge of affection went through her as she thought of his reassuring ordinariness. He would grumble at her, complain as he used to complain when they were children and he had had to rescue her from various scrapes: haul her out of the deep rock pool whose sides were too steep to climb; help her down from the garden wall where she had been practising to be a tightrope dancer; and many more.

This was by far her biggest scrape yet, but John would not fail her. Whatever steps needed taking, with lawyers, passport officials, detectives even, and with Nicolas, he would not rest until they were taken, and she was free.

For the next few days Carol waited in the hope of a cable from Rosie, or the unheralded arrival of her brother, demanding to see her. John could be stubborn, quite as stubborn as Nicolas, who could hardly refuse to let him see his own sister.

Meanwhile, she schooled herself to be charming and agreeable to all the new people she was meeting with Nicolas. She smiled, and talked, and answered their questions with a serenity which he seemed to approve. She could afford to be serene. Before long she would be back in her own surroundings; these were faces she would never see again.

During this waiting time she had no quarrel with Nicolas, who became more relaxed as the days went by. It was as if a truce had been declared, as if he had put the past out of his mind and was exerting himself to amuse and entertain—even to charm. If Carol had not been increasingly anxious over John's non-appearance, she would have found the time they spent together very pleasant. In spite of herself, she could feel the attraction of his personality still.

More than once, Carol caught herself wondering what it would be like to spend the rest of her life with a Nicolas who wanted her to be his wife because he loved her. There were moments, when she felt his eyes on her from the other side of a room full of people, or heard his laugh as Aunt Lucia teased him about his coming marriage, when she could almost imagine this was so. But imagination she knew was something which had to be kept in check, or it could run away with you.

And John did not come. Five days passed, then a week, and Carol began to think that he was ill, or that Rosie had not been able to find him, or that there was a postal strike. She tried to hide her anxiety from Nicolas, but without success.

'Is the strain of being engaged proving intolerable?' he asked.

Carol shook her head. When he smiles like that, with his eyes, she thought, he is unbearably attractive.

Nicolas had taken to coming early to fetch her from the tower, before he drove her to yet another formal family lunch party. On this occasion he had come so early that the postman arrived while he was there.

There were five or six letters, probably letters of congratulations from friends in England, but on one of them she recognised the very black ink and square shape of her brother's handwriting.

'Read them,' Nicolas said lazily. 'We have plenty of time. I can look at the sea.' His smile softened the command, but it was still a command.

And he was not, she knew, looking at the sea. She left John's letter to the last, hoping to keep it until later when she was alone, but when she had finished all the others she raised her eyes to find Nicolas studying her face with amusement.

'You have missed one,' he said.

'It's not important,' Carol said. 'I must change if I'm not to make you late.'

'I said there was time,' Nicolas said. His voice was lazy, but inflexible. 'If it's not important, it won't take long to read. Or if you like I can read it out to you while you get ready.'

Carol had no choice but to open John's letter and compose her face to read it under Nicolas's steady gaze. The letter did not take long to read. It made no mention of her letter to Rosie; there was no hint in it of any plan to come to her rescue, nor any indication that John knew anything at all about the true state of affairs between herself and the man who sat so coolly observing her. There was a PS from Rosie.

'John says he disclaims all responsibility for such a dotty sister, but I think it's wildly romantic and marvellous, and I can't wait to come and see you as a Wicked Baroness. Did he sweep you off your feet? You are a stinker, not to write and tell me all. I expect you're frantically busy, and I'll have to wait till after you're married. Anyway I'm thrilled for you . . .'

'Not bad news?' Nicolas asked, and Carol realised that her face must have shown her bewilderment.

'It's from my brother,' Carol said as lightly as she could. 'Just scolding me for the inconsiderate shortness of our engagement, and saying he can leave his conference for one day to give me away. You can read it if you like.'

Nicolas waved away the outstretched paper. 'I never read other people's letters. And that reminds me . . .' He put his hand in his pocket. 'How could I have been so forgetful? I hope *this* letter was not urgent.'

With a pang of dismay, Carol recognised her own handwriting on the bulky envelope he held out to her. It was her letter to Rosie.

His eyes were intent on her face.

'Did you read it?' Carol asked, anger choking the words.

'My dear Carol, I have just said that I do not read other people's letters.'

'But you hold them up,' said Carol.

'I thought you might have said more than you meant,' he replied smoothly. 'And then Aunt Lucia was so anxious to keep me from seeing it. I don't know what you told her, but if you thought you could pledge her to secrecy you do not know her as well as I do. Dear Aunt Lucia,' he went on, smiling, 'so full of good intentions, but you must have heard her refer to herself as a scatterbrain. And when she has a secret to hide, she behaves as if she is an undercover agent for a foreign power—everything except the cloak and dagger.'

'So you guessed . . .'

'It was quite simple. All I had to tell her was that I knew all about it already. She scolded me for a wicked devil of a nephew and said that I did not deserve a surprise wedding present from London.' He raised his eyebrows and added, 'I am curious to know what kind of a wedding present you are giving me, my dear bride, to need at least six pages'—he weighed the letter in his hand—'or seven, to go with the order.'

'Did Aunt Lucia give it to you?'

'She laughed and said that I might as well lend her a stamp, as she had run out, and I told her that as I was going to Sannat it would be the easiest thing in the world to post it for her, and you would never know.'

'Until now,' said Carol. 'How very kind. And thoughtful.'

'So do you want me to post it?' Nicolas said, still smiling.

'It's too late,' Carol answered him, and took the letter from his hand.

CHAPTER SEVEN

JOHN would not be coming. Her letter to Rosie had never left Gozo. During the luncheon which followed the discovery of these two bleak facts, Carol hid her feelings behind a mask of politeness. She hardly knew what she was eating, or what was being said to her. All she could think of was that Nicolas had behaved abominably, and that if she was to escape from the impossible position she was in, she must act now.

No longer was there any question of waiting for a good opportunity to present itself. With only a few days left, she had to make her own opportunity. If she could reach Mgarr, she could catch the ferry to Malta, but she would need money—she would have to sell her ring first. Once in Malta she could telephone John. Somehow or other he could be relied on to get her back to England, and there, surely, she would be able to find ways of straightening out the web of entanglement in which she was caught.

Carol was so angry with Nicolas that she could not trust herself to look at him. As he drove her back to the tower she was aware that he knew of her anger and was amused by it, which made her all the more determined to carry out her half-formed plan.

'You do not look well; you are so pale,' Ta Dentella said when he had gone. 'You should rest, I think.'

'No, Ta Dentella. Not rest,' said Carol. 'Fresh air, that's what I need. And some exercise. Just a little walk . . .' And before the old nurse could say more than, 'But the Baron . . .'

Carol was out of the apartment and walking down the winding road from the tower as fast as she dared. She did not want to put Ta Dentella on the alert by openly running away.

On her way along the little stony road to Sannat, a few Gozitans greeted her with their usual friendly reserve, no hint of surprise in their manner. It was almost too easy. Carol's courage mounted as the stony road became paved and led her to the main square of the town-village, where she knew there were shops.

But here she realised with dismay that her entry was becoming a matter of far too great an interest for her own good. Women looked up from their knitting. The old men under the trees nodded gravely and took off their ancient hats in solemn welcome. Small children stopped their play and stood by the side of the street, staring round-eyed.

Everyone knew who she was. It would be as mad to try to sell Nicolas's ring in Sannat as it would be to try to sell the crown jewels from the Tower of London.

But then where could she go? What could she do? Carol wondered how long it would take to walk to Victoria; there she knew she stood a better chance of selling the ring and slipping away unknown.

The sounding of a horn and a cloud of dust announced what seemed like the answer to prayer, as the old battered green bus rattled into the square and stopped only a few yards away. Carol knew that in Gozo all the roads were like the spokes of a wheel, with Victoria as the hub; to her relief Victoria was on the name board. In a moment she was sitting in one of the wooden slatted seats, trying not to notice the curious looks of the other passengers as the bus jolted and swayed along the road to the citadel.

There was an awkward minute or two when she

explained to the conductor that she had come out without her purse—would he allow her to stay on the bus? 'Of course, no problem,' he said with a smiling shrug. 'Tomorrow—any time.'

In Victoria, Carol breathed more easily. The market-place was full of stalls selling hats and mats and vegetables and souvenirs, as it had been when she and Rosie and John had visited it. Among so many tourists, she felt less conspicuous.

Beyond the marketplace were the little shops, small and dark in the tiny crooked streets. She remembered a jeweller where Rosie had looked at silver brooches, and to her relief found it without any trouble.

But when she had bent her head to duck under the low lintel, and stepped inside, she recognised at once the man who was reading a paper behind the counter. He was the very jeweller who had come to the tower to measure her finger for the diamond and sapphire ring. Carol remem-bered the morning he had come, with plain rings on a thin metal rod, graded in all sizes. While she had tried them, Nicolas had been sitting by the window, looking out to sea. Carol had thought he was bored, until he had turned suddenly, and smiled at her.

Now Carol could see that the jeweller was as surprised to see her as she was dismayed to see him. To sell a piece of jewellery to a stranger—as had been her plan—was one matter. To sell her engagement ring back to the very jeweller who had supplied it was quite another.

'But this is the greatest pleasure!' He hurried round his counter, swept the dust off a chair and stood waiting. 'What brings *madame* herself to my small shop?'

Carol was at a loss for an answer, so she sat in the chair and clasped her hands in front of her. The ring, Nicolas's ring, glinted and sparkled, accusing her.

'Yes?' said the jeweller, waiting for her to speak. 'It is beautiful, the ring—but is there something wrong? Does it not fit well? *Madame* remembers that I took such care . . .'

A voice behind Carol startled her, setting her heart pounding.

'No, no, Bartozzi, there is nothing wrong. Carol, my dear, a thousand apologies for my lateness. I was delayed.' Nicolas—for, unbelievably, it was Nicolas—laid his hand on Carol's shoulder and smiled at her, then at the jeweller.

The shock of his presence was enough to overwhelm Carol utterly. He had an almost devilish power of appearing suddenly and silently where he was least expected. It was uncanny, and at this moment devastating.

She tried to find words, any words, but Nicolas was explaining to the jeweller how it was that he had arranged to meet his fiancée after her other shopping. 'To choose a pair of earrings,' he said smoothly, 'with the same depth of colour as the sapphires in the ring—with which we are both so delighted.' He smiled down at Carol. She felt the pressure of his hand on her shoulder, and made herself nod and smile back as if in happy agreement.

'Yes, indeed,' she said. 'It is lovely.'

Carol did her best to concentrate on choosing from the trays of earrings which the jeweller drew out one after another for her to examine. But her heart was beating too fast for comfort, and she was only too aware of the tension in the tall figure beside her.

It was still there as he drove her away from the town she had thought would be her stepping-stone to freedom. But his voice was deliberately casual.

'You should have told me that you wanted to go to Victoria,' he said. 'I could have driven you. I know that

Aunt Lucia tells me I drive like the devil, but I can't believe that you prefer to be driven by a Gozitan bus-driver. That would be too great a blow to my ego.'

'How did you know?' said Carol.

'Where to find you? The whole island was ready to tell me. On my way through Sannat I was told by at least twelve people that they had seen my charming fiancée, and seven of them were intensely surprised that you were travelling by bus.'

Carol was silent. She still felt stunned.

'And then, at Bartozzi's—— My dear Carol, were you really about to try to sell the engagement ring I was at such pains to choose for you?' He glanced down at her, and Carol turned away. 'If you are so short of money, you have only to say what you want, and I will buy it for you.'

Carol found words at last. 'My plane ticket to England?' she said. 'Would you buy me that?'

It was Nicolas's turn to say nothing. He stopped the car and sat with one hand on the wheel, the other stretched out along the back of Carol's seat, not quite touching her.

'Tell me one thing,' he said, and looked very straight into her eyes. 'Is it so very terrible a prospect, to be married to me?'

When he looked at her so directly, without mockery, without arrogance, or triumph, or scorn, Carol found that she could not return his gaze and answer 'Yes'. Everything else—anxiety for the future, regret for the past, confusion about her feelings for Nicolas, and his for her—fell away before the look in those disturbingly dark eyes.

No, if she were honest with herself, she knew that it would not be a terrible thing to be married to Nicolas, not terrible at all.

But she could not tell him this at once. Her chin went up,

and she said, 'I can think of worse fates.'

'Thank you,' he said, and the corner of his mouth twitched.

'You have money. Land. Houses. A strong sense of family. What could there be for me to object to?'

'Nothing,' said Nicolas. Without warning, he took her by the shoulders, bent his head and kissed her with a deliberation and thoroughness which both surprised and shocked her. She was surprised, because she had not realised until that moment how much she had wanted him to do it. And she was shocked by the response of her own body to the force and power of such a kiss. I want you; I love you, she wanted to say. I want you to love me.

When at last he let her go, Carol felt too shaken to say anything.

'That is all I wanted to know,' said Nicolas calmly. 'I think we shall do quite well as husband and wife.'

And so it was that Carol stood once again in front of a long looking-glass while Ta Dentella arranged a wedding veil to fall in soft gossamer folds on her shoulders. But this time it was being arranged not over the short blue beach dress she had worn when she climbed the path, but over a wedding dress of finely tucked cream silk.

The veil of Gozo lace was of a greater delicacy and intricate design that anything Carol had seen outside a museum.

'It is very old, this veil,' said Ta Dentella, stroking it gently with her crooked fingers. 'It has been in the family for many generations, and it is always worn by the bride of the eldest son. That is why you wear it today.'

'It looks so fragile,' said Carol.

'Looks, yes,' the old woman agreed. 'But lace is strong.

And very—what do you say when it lasts a long, long time?'

'Enduring?' said Carol.

'That is the word. Strong and enduring, like a woman's love. Women may look weak and fragile, as lace does. But when a woman truly loves—as you do, I think—she is more strong than anyone else on the earth.'

Carol drew in a breath, and asked the question she had been wanting to ask for a long time.

'There was someone before,' she said, with a query in her voice. 'Someone he nearly married?'

'Ah, so you have heard,' said Ta Dentella, her face changing. 'It was not a good story. Very bad. But you have asked me, and I must tell you, though no one has ever spoken of it since the day she ran away. No one would dare. It was their wedding day.'

Carol waited, and after a pause Ta Dentella went on. 'No one spoke of it, but everyone remembered. And Nicolas——' Her voice dropped, and faltered.

'Who was she?' said Carol gently.

'They had been children together. She was a neighbour, Paula Hametta. They were both so young, so much in love—or so it seemed to us. To me, to his mother, to all . . .' Ta Dentella stopped once more, staring into the past.

'What went wrong?'

'It was an American, a friend from his university, who came here. He was very very rich, and he was a collector of old books. That is why he came. He heard of one old, old book, very beautiful, with pictures made by the monks. And he wanted it, to buy it. Always when he saw something beautiful he wanted to buy it.' Her voice was sad.

'And he wanted Paula?' Carol asked.

'He was a *guest* of Nicolas!' Ta Dentella said, her face

flushed in remembered indignation. 'And all three of them, the young people, they swam, and they danced, and they were very happy together. Playing music, sailing—all was pleasure. But Nicolas, he did not see that his Paula was falling in love with his friend. Perhaps she did not know it herself until it was too late. Or perhaps she knew, but she did not dare to face the truth, or she could not tell Nicolas. And then it was her wedding day, and the American took her away. So she did not have to tell Nicolas in the end.'

'Poor Nicolas,' said Carol. She saw him for the first time as a young man who could be hurt.

'Afterwards, he changed,' said Ta Dentella. 'In his heart he was not well. Before, he was like a boy. Eager, always laughing. But afterwards, he did not smile . . .' She paused. 'To other people he was always so good, but for himself—it was as if he did not care what happened to him any more.'

'I am glad you told me,' Carol said, and the old nurse smiled at her reflection in the glass.

'It is good that he has found you,' she said. 'You will make him happy again, as he used to be.'

'I shall try,' said Carol, and clung to Ta Dentella for a long moment, as if she would draw strength from the love which his old nurse felt for Nicolas.

Of the drive to the chapel, and of the ceremony itself, Carol had only a series of isolated impressions, which later stood out like snapshots in an album:

Her brother, arriving at the last minute, looking formal and unfamiliar in his solidly built morning suit, complaining—but mildly—about the heat, the rush, his conference, the inconvenience he had been put to, and Carol's sisterly lack of forethought.

'Might have given us a bit more time. Up to you and

Nick, of course. Seems like a chap who can make up his mind quickly—anyone can see that. Good organiser, too. Arranged everything for me.'

The faces which lined the road from the tower to the chapel—some she recognised. The hairdresser was there, and the shoemaker and his whole family, and the woman who had made her wedding dress. All were in their best clothes, for although they would not be in the chapel for the strictly family ceremony, they were coming to the festivities afterwards. Two little girls in matching frilly dresses threw flower petals as the car drove past them, and Carol waved.

The chapel itself, its single bell jangling—it was a tiny building, a miniature church, all pillars and domes. A basket of flowers, she noticed, by the chapel door, and a photographer on one knee, his camera aimed at her like a gun.

Then the darkness inside the chapel as she walked in beside John, away from the bright sun outside. A rustle of movement, and a turning of heads as she stood there, hesitating. The chapel was so small that it took her only a few steps to walk up the aisle and stand next to Nicolas, who stood as still as a statue of dark stone.

He did not turn his head once towards her during the ceremony, not until the priest had joined their hands and spoken the words she had already heard in Latin: 'Those whom God hath joined together let no man put asunder.'

She was not prepared for the intensity of the look Nicolas turned on her then. It was a look of victory—strangely unguarded, but possessive, too. 'You are mine,' it seemed to say, as clearly as if he had spoken the words aloud. 'To have, and to hold.' And the pressure of his hand on hers, making the ring bite into her finger, was not so fierce as that look of triumphant possession.

Afterwards, one dreamlike impression followed another.
The waft of Paris scent as the Baroness kissed Carol's cheek
and called her 'my very dear daughter'. The startling sight
of Aunt Lucia's hat, which might have been designed for a
spacewoman, quivering with vivid antennae to match her
glittering dress. The walk back through the chapel, beside
Nicolas this time, and the clicking of cameras and the blaze
of sudden sunlight, and the children lined up outside,
scattering handfuls of flower petals over them.

There were no cars to take them to the *palazzo*, although
the chapel was a little way outside the great carved
gateposts of Xatahn. Carol felt the rough stones of the long
drive under her thin shoes, and remembered with surprise
the time she had run there, barefoot, her only thought to
escape from the man at whose side she now walked, the man
who was now in truth her husband.

A surge of happiness and excitement swept through her,
and again she gave herself up to the sights and sounds
which surrounded her: the people—so many people, lining
the drive, filling the courtyard, milling round the trestle
tables set up in the long gardens below the terrace, and
Nicolas leading her forward as if to present her to them all.
The fine-stemmed glass of champagne someone pushed into
her hand—the sound of music—the talking and laughing
which floated up like the noise of the sea—the sight of the
town band in ribboned hats. The feel of Nicolas's hand on
her elbow, steering her down the steps and through the
waves of guests—and everywhere smiles, and greetings,
and laughter.

'You will be very happy with such a fine husband,' said a
short, wiry man Carol recognised as the man who had
driven one of the donkey carts in the carnival. 'And you,

my lord, will be pleased, too.' He added a string of words in
Maltese which made Nicolas laugh, and allow his hand to
be shaken with vigour.

'What did he say?' Carol asked, and Nicolas laughed
again.

'He said that I would be pleased to have such a beautiful
wife to love me, and give me many strong children.'

'At least he didn't say, "And may they all be sons!"' said
Aunt Lucia, appearing beside them with a plate of food.
'*Biskuttini*,' she explained to Carol. 'Very special, for
weddings and christenings only. My dear girl, has no one
given you anything to eat? Even brides can't live on love
alone. Nicolas, the poor child will faint.'

Nicolas glanced quickly at Carol, and she knew that he
was remembering the film wedding when he answered,
'Not this time, I think.' Aunt Lucia, all unaware, told him
he was a dreadful nephew, and she pitied Carol from the
bottom of her heart for having to put up with him for any
longer than a day, let alone a lifetime.

All through the eating and drinking, the greeting of
guests and the shaking of hands, the speeches and the
commendations, Carol smiled, and nodded, and looked as
radiant as a young and beautiful bride should look on the
happiest day of her life. And Nicolas, by her side, always by
her side, was everything that a good bridegroom should
be—attentive and proudly possessive, guarding her as if she
were some precious and exquisite jewel which he had long
wanted and at last secured for his own.

The darkness fell about them like a cloak, and the moon
rose. Lanterns were lit among the branches of the flowering
trees, and the band trooped up the stone steps to the terrace
and through the long windows into the house.

'It is time for the dancing to begin,' said Nicolas, and he

looked down at Carol with a light in his eyes which made Aunt Lucia sigh and say to the Baroness that anyone could see that darling Nicolas was hopelessly *épris*, and how thankful they all must be that he could be happy at last. Carol, glancing up, saw the fire in his look, and caught her breath. It was difficult to believe that this tall, proud, difficult and commanding man was her husband.

'The custom is for us to lead the way,' he said, and took her hand in his.

In the main salon of the *palazzo*, the rugs had been taken up and the marble floor was a smooth as glass. Afterwards, Carol could not have said how long they danced, whether it was for minutes or for hours. All she knew was that Nicolas held her as firmly, but also as gently, as if she were a flower that would snap. She was surprised that so tall a man could be so light on his feet.

The floor helped, and so did the champagne, she imagined. Marble was a surface on which to glide and whirl, and turn, and skim, and twirl again. But dancing with Nicolas was like nothing she had done before. All the partners she had ever had, in that long-ago time of life-before-marriage, had danced moderately well, but their dancing had been a polite shuffle compared with this.

With Nicolas she really danced, with a grace and a joyfulness of movement which was new to her. With him, she realised, it was a grace imbued with an underlying power, and Carol responded to it with exhilaration.

The strangest part of it was that the other people surrounding them on the dance floor might have been wraiths for all that they seemed to count. Carol felt, for the first time that day, that she was quite alone with Nicolas. No one else mattered; only they were reality. Everything else about them—the lights in the trees outside, the servants tidying up in the garden, the old ladies nodding their heads on the terrace, the uncles discussing politics by the door, the fiddler working himself into a frenzy, the drummer reaching for the glass under his chair, the other couples— all these were dream stuff. Only she and Nicolas were real.

Being so close to him, like this, made it easier to accept the possibility that he loved her, that their marriage was not a game, that they could be happy together. Never had she been so conscious of the nearness of a man as she was of Nicolas's arm round her waist, of his face above hers.

'Well, my wife,' he said, and there was an ironic lift to the corner of his mouth. 'Is this wedding more to your liking than your last?'

Carol tilted her face to look up at him. Speaking lightly, though her heart cried out, don't hurt me, she said, 'You'll have a perfect excuse for forgetting which day is our anniversary,' at which Nicolas threw back his head and laughed.

'"To have and to hold",' he quoted. 'Almost the same as the family motto: "What I hold, I hold dear." How many anniversaries do you look forward to? Thirty, forty, fifty? We're both reasonably young and quite healthy. The dancing, in the old days, was a way of making that evident to all.'

'I thought it was to keep warm,' said Carol, keeping her voice light, 'in draughty old castles. And something to do in the evenings before television was invented.'

'That's only part of it,' said Nicolas. 'It was really a shop-window affair, a way of parading the wares a woman had to offer. Her father could haggle over the dowry, but she had to show what else she could produce in more physical terms. If she danced well, it was a sign of how supple she was, how good she would be in the marriage bed.'

He held her a little way from him then, and swept an amused glance over her, taking her in from head to foot before he drew her to him again. Much to her annoyance, Carol felt the blood rush up into her throat and face, and knew that Nicolas had seen her blush.

'A blushing bride,' he said 'How very fortunate I am! But you don't say if you agree with me?'

'How can I?' said Carol, with spirit. 'You might just as well say that if two people danced well together, that would show they would get on well in life.'

'And do we dance well together, my twice-married wife, my enchanting Calypso?' said Nicolas, whirling her out beyond the pillars which marked the edge of the salon, and on to the now deserted terrace.

Carol could not answer, but looked down, afraid that he would find out from her eyes how much she loved him, and how much she longed and hoped for him to love her in return.

'A modest wife,' he said, and laughed shortly. 'There is a time for modesty, too, but not now. Come. It is time we left the revellers to their revelling. If we don't leave them, in fact, they will begin to wonder why we married at all.'

'Now? Like this?' said Carol. 'Without saying goodbye to anyone?'

'Yes,' said Nicolas. 'We'll cut the farewells. I have told my mother, and she agrees.'

He took her hand and led her through a side door in the high stone wall of the gardens. On the other side, in the narrow track-like road, his red car waited for them. In a moment he was in the driving seat, and Carol beside him; in another, the lights and the music of the *palazzo* were behind them and only the moon and the stars kept them company as the headlights carved a way through the night.

'Where are we going? Not back to the tower?' said Carol, catching at the flying ends of her veil and trying to hold them round her shoulders.

'Back to prison?' he said. 'No, my poor caged bird. Now there is no need. No. Where is most fitting for Calypso, on Calypso's island, but the villa next door to her cave?'

'But,' said Carol, astonished, 'it was only half built.'

'It is finished now. As yet no one has slept in it. We shall be the first.' He looked down at her quickly, and away. 'It is a new venture. I propose to let it for large sums of money in the holiday season. In time, it will probably be overlaid with the trappings of tourism. Beach umbrellas will be hired from it, and people will drink cocktails with barbaric names at little tables on the terrace. But tonight it is ours, and ours alone. The staff are all enjoying themselves. We left them dancing in the gardens of Xatahn.'

The car stopped, and the silence of the night was filled with the singing of a thousand cicadas.

To Carol, it was like being taken back in time. Once more, the nearly full moon made a path of silver on the dark waters of Ramla Bay. Once more, she heard the far-off whisper of the waves and smelt a waft of thyme and fennel from the hillside. Once more, Nicolas stood before her, a hand's breadth away.

The last time they had stood there, so close, but not touching, her mind and body had ached with a longing for him to take her in his arms. It did not need memory to bring back that longing. She shut her mind to the past and the future, and thought only of Nicolas standing there, and herself, and the sea below.

He made a move towards her, and checked himself. 'Not yet,' he said. 'Not here. Ceremonies are made to be observed. Thresholds are there to be crossed.'

Swiftly, without another word, he picked her up and carried her over to the entrance of the villa. Carol was barely aware of the pillars surrounding the inner court-yard, of the wide-stepped stairs of pale marble where Nicolas carried her, silent in his arms, to the great balconied room above, the moon making white bars through the unshuttered windows.

Still in silence, he set her on her feet and stood facing her.

'Calypso,' he said, and stretched out his hand to her face, fingering the lace of the veil against her cheek. 'My Calypso.'

Slowly, one by one, he loosened the pins which held the veil in place, and let them drop to the floor. At last the veil, too, fell away, and lay, a white shadow on the moon-streaked marble, forgotten by them both.

CHAPTER EIGHT

CAROL woke next morning to the small sounds of household activity: the soft sweeping of the terrace under the window, subdued kitchen noises of china and spoons and saucepans. She wondered when the servants had come back, and lay with her eyes shut, remembering the passion and the joy of the night, aware of her own body as she had never been before.

She was almost reluctant to wake up. What could be said after such a night? How would she look to Nicolas? How would they look to each other in the clear light of the morning?

He must still be asleep. Carol reached out an arm, and opened her eyes to find that she was alone in the wide bed. Only a hollowed pillow and a rumpled sheet showed that Nicolas had lain beside her.

Carol smiled. She did not see Nicolas as minding whether she saw him unshaven or tousle-haired, but he might well have decided to swim in the bay below, or walk, or run. How little she knew him, and how much there was to learn.

She was filled with a deep contentment such as she had never known, and knew that it was because, to her amazement and delight, she was loved by the man she had fallen in love with first on the magic day of the carnival.

For of this she was sure. No man could have made love with such tenderness within the passion, such a blend of longing, triumph and gentleness, unless he were in love. The last three weeks of confusion, suspicion and doubt were swept away as by a fierce fire. What remained was pure happiness. She and Nicolas were married. They loved one another.

It was almost too good to be true, like a fairy story where all there was left for the characters to do at the end was to be happy ever after. And that, Carol felt, would be all the more wonderful for the difficulties and misunderstandings which had gone before.

A soft knock interrupted her thoughts, and her 'come in' was followed by the entry of a young girl Carol recognised as one of Ta Dentella's great-nieces, Jessy. She was carrying a tray with great care, and set it down on a table by the bed.

'Shall I pour the coffee for you, *madame?*' she said.

'Thank you, Jessy,' said Carol, and then, noticing that the tray was laid for one, asked, 'Has Nicolas—has the Baron had his breakfast already?'

'Oh, I think he does not breakfast,' said the girl, hesitantly. 'He go very early. He does not want to wake you. He give orders not to wake *madame* until nine.'

Go? Carol was not prepared for the shock which the word gave her, but then realised Jessy must mean that he had gone out, perhaps to swim, as she had first thought. She was sorry he had not woken her. She would have liked to be with him, to do what he was doing, on their first morning of true, unspoiled happiness.

She wanted to ask where he had gone, and why, and when he would be back, but pride checked her. If she, Nicolas's newly married wife, did not know why he had gone out so early, then it would seem very strange.

'Of course,' she said instead. 'I remember. Thank you, Jessy,' and smiled at the girl as she hurried away.

After her coffee and a leisurely bath, Carol put on a pale blue skirt and a white silk shirt, knowing that they set off the brown of her skin and the fairness of her hair. Nicolas might come back at any moment. She wanted to look her best.

It was when she came downstairs to the big sitting-room, with its one wall open to the terrace and the view, that she saw the square white envelope on the writing desk. At first, when she saw the name, thickly scrawled in Nicolas's handwriting, she thought it must be a letter for his mother. 'The Baroness of Xatahn,' she read. It was a full minute before she remembered that it was her own name now.

Carol was puzzled. What could he have to write to her about when they would be seeing one another within minutes? She opened the letter and began to read.

Even then, her mind would not let her see the truth. She had to read it over and over again before the chill, sardonic words had any meaning for her.

'My charming Calypso,' it began.

'Now that there can be no question of an annulment—after a consummation which I think you will agree was beyond dispute—you no longer have any ground for blackmail, or any kind of a hold on me, beyond the normal ones of matrimony.

'You may not have realised that it mattered little to me whether I was married or not. The only fear I had was that you would cause a scandal which would hurt my mother, my name, and my family.

'I hope you will excuse me, my dear enchantress, for being so carried away by your touching beauty, and the importance of the occasion, that I displayed rather more of that famous charm I once warned you about than I intended. You need not fear that I hold you in any more than the respect you deserve—you are quite a worthy opponent—or that I shall embarrass you by making further unnecessary claims upon you as my wife.

'It may come as a relief to you to learn that I have to go to Valletta. You can tell everyone that it is an urgent crisis in my agricultural affairs, which will earn you their sympathy, I am sure. It is probably best for all concerned that my return is "unavoidably delayed" until you have moved back into our quarters in Xatahn.

'Until then, salutations from your devoted husband, Nicolas.'

Carol stood perfectly still, the letter in her hand. At first she was unable to believe the words on the page. Over and over again she read them, punishing herself with their stark message, their cynical denial of everything she had thought there was between herself and Nicolas.

'A consummation which I think you will agree was beyond dispute . . .'—as if it had been a deliberate act of strategy—'mattered little to me whether I was married or not . . . displayed rather more of that famous charm . . .'

Everything—his dancing, his words and gestures, the tone of his voice, the closeness, the touch of his hands—everything, *everything* had been a deliberate exercise of his charm, spiced no doubt by genuine desire. The physical desire had been real; he could hardly have faked that. But the tenderness, the words he had murmured, all that she had thought of as love—all of it had been just part of an act, a performance.

And then to go away, to leave her, the day after their

wedding! If it was in retribution for the hurt which had been done to him, so long ago, why should he do it to her? It was not fair, she thought, passionately repeating the childish words in her mind, not *fair*, when her only fault had been to love him.

Her first instinct was that of an animal which has been wounded and flies to a place of solitude. But here, in this strange villa, in this alien island, on a day which looked already as if it were painted in brilliant enamel on the face of the hard-hearted rock, where could she fly? Here she was already alone, quite alone. Nicolas had gone, and she knew, for certain, that he did not love her, never had loved her, and never would.

Her despair was total, devastating. It was followed by a feeling of cold fury. How dared he treat her with such callous unconcern? What right had he to assume so much that was wrong, and refuse ever to listen to the truth?

When he came back—for come back he must, to save his precious pride—she would be twice as cold and distant as he evidently meant to be. If revenge and rejection were the only emotions he recognised, then she would have to learn to feel and use them, too. It had been so easy, all too easy, to fall in love with Nicolas. She would have to school her heart to fall out of love.

Love was only an emotion, like any other: jealousy, or greed, or anger. Like them, it could be controlled. It could be damped down, stamped upon, and in time killed. Half the killing, Carol told herself, was done already, by the letter she held in her hand.

She tore the letter across and across, and then shredded all the fragments until they were no larger than crumbs, and scattered them over the balustrade of the terrace, to drift down in the breeze and settle in among the wild flowers below. In the heat of the sun, she noticed, the vivid blue of the thistles had faded to grey. The tall grasses were dried to a brittle spikiness. There was no smell of thyme in the air.

Carol spent the week of her honeymoon alone, writing thank-you letters to Nicolas's many friends and relations, and to those few friends of hers who had seen the announcement in *The Times*, and written to wish her every happiness. Anger with Nicolas, and a stubborn pride of her own, kept her from breaking down. She had summoned Jessy and told her that the Baron had been called away on very urgent and important business, and impressed upon her that no member of the family must learn of this because of the anxiety it would cause them.

She must tell no one, not even her great-aunt. Ta Dentella had gone to visit her sister in Malta; Carol missed her soothing company, but was thankful that she did not have to face the questions and the concern of the old lace-maker.

It would have been impossible for Carol to go to Xatahn until the end of the supposed honeymoon. She had already said her goodbyes to Nicolas's mother, who would still be packing up her own possessions and making arrangements for her move to Victoria.

'I feel that we are chasing you out of your own home,' Carol had said, but the Baroness had laughed.

'There is a saying here,' she said. '"The new nail drives out the old one"; but in my case the old nail does not want to stay for ever in the same plank of wood. And I know myself, my dear,' she had continued, stopping Carol's protests, 'if I were here, in Gozo, I should be for ever wanting to give you good advice, and before long you

would be thinking me a tiresome old autocrat, and secretly
longing for me to take myself off.'

When the day arrived for Carol to return to Xatahn, to
take her place in the *palazzo* as its new mistress, she would
have welcomed all the advice that anyone would have been
prepared to give her.

Her first ordeal was that she would be returning alone.
She had heard nothing of or from Nicolas, nor had she
expected to. 'You're on your own,' she told herself
bracingly, but could not help feeling nervous as she saw
Charles, the old Baroness's driver, pull up outside the villa
at the appointed time. As Nicolas's mother was making a
tour of visits to her own family and friends in Paris and
Rome before settling down in her town house in Victoria,
she had put her car and driver at Carol's disposal. Charles
was to help with the luggage. He showed no surprise at
Nicolas's absence.

'The Baron will drive himself home,' Carol told him in as
confident a voice as she could summon. 'He had very
important business to deal with today, and he will come as
soon as he is free.'

And I hope that is true, she thought. What she would do
if he did not come she did not know. Her immediate
concern was the welcome she might expect from the staff at
the *palazzo*. As a foreigner, an unknown girl from no great
family, she could not see how they could think very much of
her, especially as she was taking the place of a mistress
whom they had loved and respected, and who was, besides,
a member of the old nobility.

Reserve there certainly was, as Carol saw from the
moment she stepped out of the car on that first day. But she
had already learnt that Gozitans do not give their affection

easily to the strangers who came to their island. She did not know that the servants at Xatahn had already made up their minds about her. They loved the old Baroness, but they saw how freely she welcomed Carol into the family. More important still, the young Baron had chosen her to be his bride, and therefore she must be an exceptional person, and one worthy of their respect and love.

Cassar the gardener greeted Carol with a saying in Maltese which she did not understand, and a spray of flowers.

'Thank you,' Carol said. 'What a lovely scent!'

'I translate for you,' the old man said. 'It is a saying: "What a new bride touches",' and his wrinkled face broke into a smile, '"smells good."'

'If you give me flowers like these to touch, then it is true,' said Carol.

Cassar was much readier to show her his gardens, nurseries and the glasshouses which lined the high walls below the terrace, than Anna was to show her the kitchens. Anna, the cook, was a square-set woman with gold earrings and a way of planting her feet firmly as she walked about her kitchens. These remote, mysterious rooms at the back of the *palazzo* were her kingdom. Although she was officially the cook, she also held complete sway over an irregular army of young women—nieces, cousins and others who came to keep the rooms clean, and wash the clothes, and help her when she needed extra hands to peel vegetables or skim the stockpot.

'How many for supper, *madame*?' she asked Carol, who could not decide whether the look in Anna's eye was quizzical, pitying or simply enquiring. She straightened her back and spoke with a decision which seemed advisable in the new Baroness of Xatahn.

'Two,' she said firmly, 'unless the Baron is further delayed. What are his favourite dishes?'

Carol could not have thought of a better way to break through Anna's guard. At first hesitantly, and then in a growing flood of information, she told Carol that from a small boy he had always loved *torta tar rikotta*, and that now he never failed to praise her grilled swordfish. When at last she disappeared to her stronghold, she left Carol to sit in the cool, high-ceilinged drawing-room and wonder when Nicolas would come.

Nicolas did not come. Aunt Lucia arrived, in her small yellow car and a silk suit with a jazzy print reminiscent of forked lightning. She embraced Carol warmly and did not even notice Nicolas's absence.

'Never ask anyone about honeymoons,' she said briskly. 'Are you well? That's all that really matters. If I know my nephew he'll be off and busy with his own concerns, and the last thing you want to do is float about an empty house ordering the servants about. House runs as smoothly as a luxury liner anyway, and Anna won't want you poking your nose in her cooking pots. You can't spend your days arranging flowers, so you'll do much better to come out with me.'

Carol did not refuse. After her week of solitude she was relieved to be driven off by Aunt Lucia in her dashing little car, and listen to her voluble flow of talk.

'They depend on tourists to buy,' she told Carol, swerving sharply to avoid a group of women knitting at the side of the road. 'But how many big sweaters can a tourist put in her suitcase? I am trying to work out a mail order scheme.'

'What about wool supplies?' Carol asked. 'I haven't seen any sheep.' She looked about her at the stone-walled fields and rocky hillsides, where all the colour of the spring had already been turned to a monotonous yellowish grey.

'This isn't England,' said Aunt Lucia. 'No lush green fields full of white woolly sheep. They're here, though, in those fields you think are all rocks and stones. Here we are—first stop the craft village.'

The little car spun through the tall gates of what looked more like a light industrial estate than a village, and Aunt Lucia laughed at Carol's astonishment.

'It may look unromantic,' she said, 'but it's practical. Good working conditions, too—more space than in a cottage.' She whisked Carol into a high and airy building, full of light from big windows and with a number of looms. The girl working at one of these greeted Aunt Lucia warmly and, as they discussed orders and prices, Carol looked about her, admiring the soft thick rugs in pale natural colours which hung on the walls.

'It's a co-operative now,' Aunt Lucia said, as they drove off again. Nicolas calls it my crafts work, but it isn't mine really, you know. I'm just a link-woman.'

'You seem to enjoy it,' Carol said.

'I adore it!' Aunt Lucia said, narrowly missing a pile of building blocks as she turned her head towards Carol. 'It began with one spinner, and her daughter who knitted. I helped them with wool supplies—made a deal with a tenant of Nicolas for his fleeces—and it snowballed. I can't tell you how many are involved now, nor how many outlets. But it keeps me busy, I can tell you that.'

Carol could well believe it. The afternoon passed quickly, and it was nearly six when Aunt Lucia brought her back to the *palazzo*.

'I'll drag you out again,' she promised. 'I want to pick your brains about export . . .' She kissed Carol's cheek, refused her offer of a glass of sherry, and shot off down the long drive, leaving a plume of yellow dust behind her.

When it cleared, Carol saw Nicolas's red car coming towards her.

There was no time to retreat, to run upstairs, to compose her face and her thoughts, to decide what she should say, or to try to control the stupid hammering of her heart.

The car was drawing up beside the wide flight of steps where Carol had stood to wave to Aunt Lucia. Nicolas must have seen her; to run away now would look undignified. It would also give him the satisfaction of knowing that he could upset her, when her whole object was to show him that nothing he did or said could make the slightest difference to her, ever again.

All the same, it needed an intense effort of will to gather herself together and face Nicolas with composure. As he looked up at her, his whole manner was casual, relaxed, as if to have left his wife on the morning after their wedding was the most normal thing in the world.

Carol hardly took in what Nicolas was saying. She heard only her own voice, making polite enquiries about his journey, asking if the ferry had been on time, remarking on the heat of the day. At the same time, she kept an expression of pleasant indifference on her face, hoping that she looked as calm as she would have liked to feel.

To all of this Nicolas replied gravely, keeping his eyes on her face in the most unsteadying way. His own expression revealed nothing, neither remorse for what he had done, nor pleasure at seeing her again. There was only a slight air of sardonic amusement, as if he recognised the social game she was playing, and accepted it as a useful face-saving stratagem for both of them.

Despite Carol's intention to remain perfectly unconcerned as to what Nicolas thought of her, she was thankful that the sleeveless linen dress she had been wearing for her outing with Aunt Lucia had survived uncreased, and that its colour, a pale blue-green, would be helping to make her look reasonably cool and poised.

'Are you well?' said Nicolas, as Aunt Lucia had done, but Aunt Lucia had not looked her up and down appraisingly, with eyes so dark that Carol could not read what lay behind them. She had to turn her head so that he would not see the tell-tale red flooding into her cheeks.

'I must tell Anna you are here,' she said. 'She will be overjoyed to see you. She has promised to have dinner ready at eight.'

'And you?' he said. 'Are you overjoyed to see me?'

'But of course,' she answered lightly over her shoulder as she walked away. 'What else would you expect?'

That first dinner with Nicolas seemed to set the seal upon the kind of life they were destined to lead. They talked of trivialities—the flowers Cassar had brought in for the table, the postcard Ta Dentella had sent from Malta.

Then, and later, it was as if they had taken up positions of guarded neutrality towards one another. Carol was careful to say nothing which could lead Nicolas to suppose that she had ever been in any danger of falling in love with him. Not once did Nicolas refer to the cruel letter which had laid waste all her hopes and shattered her dreams of happiness with him. He told her nothing of where he had gone when he left her, nor what he had been doing during the week he was away.

As the pattern of their everyday life became set, Carol realised that she rarely saw Nicolas alone. In the morning he had his breakfast early, on the balcony of the room next to her own.

'The old Baron, may God rest his soul, and the Baroness—they had their own bedchambers,' Anna had told Carol when she showed her new mistress all the rooms of the house. 'And with the door between, they could be together or apart, as they wanted.'

And Nicolas would not want, Carol thought, as she woke every morning in the great double bed which had belonged to the Baroness, and in which she, too, had spent so many years alone. The door between their rooms was not locked; that would have made the servants aware that all was not well with the Baron and his beautiful young wife. But Nicolas kept the word he had so coldly given in his letter, and the great gilded door, crowned with cherubs and carved with leaves and fruit, remained as shut as if it had been triple locked and barred.

Sometimes Carol heard him moving about on the other side, but usually he had left the *palazzo* long before she was up. When he did return, at sunset, or later, they very often dined out. When they did not, there was hardly an evening when there were not as many as twelve, sixteen or more round the long polished table, set with a battery of silver and glass, and lit by candles which shook their flames gently in the draught of the overhead fans.

Sitting at one end of the table, Carol felt herself separated from Nicolas by a far greater distance than the two rows of guests eating and talking between them. And yet, all the time she was paying polite attention to the elderly uncle on her right, or to the solid businessman on her left, she was vividly aware of him, of his dark presence. She had to steel herself now to hear his laugh without minding, to see him smile and bend his head to respond to his neighbour, a woman whose white skin made Carol think of magnolia petals against the low-cut black silk of her dress.

'I hear that Lucia is embroiling you in her schemes,' the uncle was saying, 'and dragging you about all over the countryside.' Carol said that she liked being embroiled, and began to tell him about the craftworkers and the plans she and Aunt Lucia were making, but after listening indulgently for half a minute, he cut her short.

'My dear,' he said. 'I do not know how Nicolas feels about this kind of thing, but if I were in his shoes, I should not be happy that you spend so much time outside your own house.'

'Oh?' said Carol, keeping the smile on her face with an effort. 'He has made no objection to me.'

'The indulgence of youth,' said the uncle, quite insufferably, Carol thought. 'But I, as a senior member of the family, offer you a word of advice. You may know that we have a rich store of local sayings, in Gozo, and the one which applies to you, my dear, is this: "As the candle stands in the lantern, so the bride stays in her house." Old-fashioned, but, if you will forgive me, apt.'

Carol did not feel like forgiving him. 'You really think,' she said, 'that it's better to sit twiddling my thumbs in the house than to be out helping Aunt Lucia?' She had raised her voice more than she meant, and all the faces at the table were turned towards her. Nicolas looked at her with an expression of amusement, and the woman sitting next to him leaned forward to answer.

'Not twiddling your thumbs, surely?' she cried. 'There must be masses to do in a house like this. Flowers to arrange. Menus to plan. The servants to complain about. And then later on, of course, when there are children, you won't have a moment to call your own.'

She said something to Nicolas in a low-voiced aside, and Carol felt her cheeks reddening. What would be the reaction if she announced that, as things stood between herself and Nicolas, there would be no likelihood of children at any time?

'Do you mean,' she said, feeling her temper rising but unable to check it, 'that life holds nothing beyond flower-arranging and children? This is exactly what Aunt Lucia has done her best to change. She told me one of your splendid local sayings, too: "Feed your girls on bread-crumbs, and bid them stay in the corner." Is that where you think women should spend their lives? In the corner, out of the way?'

The woman in the black dress surveyed her from under her long—probably false, Carol thought—eyelashes, and said smoothly that corners were only for little girls and dunces, and there were other and better places for a wife to be.

There was a general laugh and for a moment Carol wondered if the other woman knew about the closed door between the two bedrooms and was deliberately taunting her. She must not lose her temper. Reminding herself that there were rules of hospitality which she as a hostess must observe, she said with a smile,

'But of course you are right. The proper place for a perfect wife is on a pedestal, so that all may admire. But how uncomfortable! Don't you agree?'

And this time the laughter was louder and friendlier, and on her side.

'I congratulate you, my dear,' Nicolas said, when all the guests had gone. 'Julia Gauci d'Elvidia is not used to losing her verbal battles.'

'I hope I wasn't rude to her,' said Carol.

'Only by chance, not by design,' Nicolas told her. 'You were not to know that she is far from being a perfect wife, and that a pedestal is the last place anyone—least of all her husband—would put her.'

It was only later, when she was alone, that Carol wondered how he knew, and whether Julia was one of the women Nicolas had made love to. Oh well, she told herself, the women Nicolas had made love to—and there must have been many—were nothing to her. As the cool uncaring wife Carol had set herself to be now, there was no place for jealousy in her range of emotions. Besides, she was much too busy to wonder what Nicolas had done in the past, or might be doing now.

Carol made a special point of being busy. She threw herself into all Aunt Lucia's plans for the craftworkers with an enthusiasm which would have shocked the elderly uncle as it delighted Aunt Lucia, and seemed to leave Nicolas unmoved.

Every day they criss-crossed the island in Aunt Lucia's tireless little car, taking orders out to a group of girls in the north, bringing fresh supplies of wool to the old ladies who sat by the roadside with their spinning wheels, transporting batches of finished garments to the show-room in the craft village, and displaying others in the market place in Victoria.

'I want to expand the range of designs,' said Aunt Lucia, 'and find new outlets. You can help me.'

And when Carol protested that she was a fabric designer, not a weaver or knitter, Aunt Lucia swept aside her protests with an impatient snort.

'No matter!' she said. 'You have the gift of creative design. You know about colours. You have an instinct for what women will wear. I have seen your new sketches; they are fabulous.'

Carol was pleased with them, too. She had drawn largely

on the flowers of the island for her inspiration for the next Célie et Cie collection: those which grew wild, and also those which Cassar tended lovingly in the gardens of Xatahn.

While she sat and drew, or painted, Cassar was busy arranging his pots of young shrubs to stand in the shade. 'This is my nursery,' he told Carol with pride, pointing to the neat rows of tiny palm trees, the scarlet trumpets of hibiscus, the blue flowers of young plumbago. 'They are my children now. I feed them; I give them water; I keep them from being burnt by the sun. And then how will they repay me?'

'By growing tall and beautiful?' Carol said.

'As the Baron's children will also, when the time comes,' said the old gardener. 'I tell you something, Madame Baroness,' and he straightened his back and looked hard at Carol. 'It is what we say here: "He who has children has a valley full of joy." And it is very wise, very true. A woman should have children, or how can she make her husband truly happy?'

Carol pressed so hard with the pencil she was using that the point broke. Happiness was for other people, but she could not tell Cassar this. How could she explain that joy of this kind—of any kind—could never come to the present Baron and Baroness of Xatahn?

CHAPTER NINE

THE days grew hotter, the blue sky harder, an upturned bowl of blue enamel. On the rare occasions when Carol and Nicolas were alone together, he treated her with controlled politeness, and she responded with a calm indifference which matched, even surpassed, his own.

'How have you spent your day?' he would enquire punctiliously. 'Profitably? You do not find it too boring, being mistress of Xatahn?'

'Not in the least,' Carol would say airily, and launch into a flippant picture of her and Aunt Lucia's doings which made him smile, in spite of himself. And when in return Nicolas told her that he had made some progress in his irrigation plans, she would say, 'Oh yes?' with so little show of interest that he would fall silent. Secretly she longed to ask a hundred questions, and to hear, as she once might have done, his enthusiastic answers.

Carol's defiant plan to show him that she did not care one snap of the fingers for him was only half successful. She might make Nicolas believe it, but herself she knew she could not deceive. Every day, living in the same house, sleeping under the same roof, she longed for things to be different, to be as she had once imagined they could be.

The strain of trying to make her heart obey her will began to tell on her health, or so Carol supposed. It might have been the heat which made her feel dizzy, and sometimes a little sick.

Anna saw that the young Baroness showed signs of tiredness when Carol said that she could not decide on menus, and would leave the choice of dishes to her. 'You have such good ideas, Anna,' she said, 'and it's too early in the morning to think about food.'

Aunt Lucia noticed the shadows under her eyes, and told her that she must not let being married to Nicolas tire her. 'Save some of your energy for our new publicity scheme. I want to pick your brains again!'

Carol tried to rouse herself from the lethargy which threatened to overcome her mind as well as her body.

'You should rest, *madame*,' Jessy said timidly. 'In the afternoons it is siesta time.' But Carol could not bear the thought of lying on her bed on those increasingly hot and languid afternoons.

Instead, she took to driving herself out in the old Baroness's stately black car, revisiting all the places she had been to with Nicolas, but they were not joyful expeditions.

When she went to the ancient salt pans at Marsalforn, she saw them as flat and empty and dried up as her love for Nicolas would be, she supposed, in time. The dark silhouette of Fungus Rock, so high and inaccessible that no one now could climb it, symbolised his remoteness; for Nicolas, who lived—or existed—so near her, might yet have been a thousand miles away for all that they had to do with one another.

Once, in Victoria, she saw him. He was talking to someone in a car, and by the way he was smiling down at the person, whoever it was, she guessed that it was a woman. It was only for a moment that Carol stood watching. When the car moved off, she recognised Julia Gauci d'Elvidia in the driving seat. She was smiling, too.

Praying that neither of them had seen her, Carol retreated into the cathedral where she joined a party of tourists who were being shown the painted dome.

'It is not a true dome,' said the guide. 'They had not

enough money for that. So a famous artist painted this ceiling to look like the inside of a dome. Do you see the small lizard down at one side?'

'It looks so real,' said one of the tourists.

'But it is only a sham,' said the guide.

'A very clever fake.' Nicolas's voice startled her. He was standing close behind her. He must have seen her, after all, and followed her in. 'Don't you agree?'

'Like so many things in life,' Carol said swiftly, lightly, as if it did not matter. 'Like marriages, for instance. The picture so often looks wonderful, but on closer inspection there's nothing there.'

For a moment only she thought that she had touched a nerve. A sudden flash of emotion came into his eyes, but in another second he had relaxed.

'You should be a connoisseur in such matters,' he said casually.

'Such matters?' Carol asked. 'Do you mean pictures, fakes, or marriage?'

'Ah, that I leave you to work out yourself,' said Nicolas, and changed the subject abruptly. 'Did you not see me down in the street? Were you trying to avoid me?' He said nothing of the Gauci woman, and Carol was too proud to ask about her.

'Not at all,' she said. 'I came in here to be cool. It was so very hot out there.'

Nicolas turned his head quickly and scrutinised her face.

'You look very pale,' he said, and Carol winced at the note of pretended concern in his voice. 'Are you sure you are well?'

'Would it worry you if I weren't?' she asked, and added carelessly, 'I can't imagine why it should.'

As she spoke, she gazed up at the false dome with great concentration, so did not see the expression in his eyes, nor did she see the line of his jaw tighten.

'You are forgetting the vigilant Aunt Lucia,' he said. 'We cannot have her scolding me for not taking care of you as well as she thinks I should.'

Carol stopped gazing at the dome, and looked squarely at Nicolas. 'How could she come to that conclusion?' she said. 'I should have thought that I had been very well taken care of, very well indeed.' You charmed me into marrying you, she wanted to say. You made me think you loved me. You let me believe that we had found great happiness in one another. You painted a wonderful picture of love—our love—and then you showed me it was false, as false as the dome up there!

But she said none of this. Instead she said, 'I should consider myself well provided for. A beautiful house; an exchanting garden; a husband whom all Gozo loves and admires. What more could I possibly ask?'

Although she tried to keep her voice light and casual, there was a shake in it which she was afraid would give her away. Whatever happened, Nicolas must never know that he had the power to hurt her, must never suspect how completely he had wrecked the illusion of happiness he had so skilfully and remorselessly built up. Praying that her face would not betray her, she turned away, looking at her watch.

'Heavens, it's late!' she said, and almost ran out of the great door of the cathedral and down the wide stone steps. Nicolas could not have followed, even if he had wished to; a coachload of schoolchildren was already jamming the entrance to the citadel as Carol hurried to her car.

She must drive somewhere, do something, anything, rather than brood over what might have been. She would go out to the cliffs at Ta Cenc and defy all the ghosts and feelings of the past.

Carol parked the car and walked out towards where the ancient cart tracks ran out to the very edge of the great cliffs. With all the caravans gone and the fence taken down, it was a wild and grand place, suiting her mood. The flowers which had covered the stony fields in a coloured tapestry now clothed them in a dead grey mat. The feathery green plumes of the fennel were spiky skeletons. Only the grey prickly pear which grew above the rubble walls was alive, but then it was armoured with a tough leathery skin, and thorns.

'That's what my heart ought to be like,' Carol told herself. 'Armoured, like a prickly pear.' Perhaps in time it would grow its own armour. And then which would be worse? The deadness of not caring, or the sharp pain like the one she felt when she saw Nicolas laughing down into the face of another woman?

Of course he would have other women. Nicolas was no monk. He was, as she knew so well, a man who could make love with passion and fierce joy. Why should she have thought that by shutting the door on her he would shut it on all women? Why should it matter to her?

It was the first time Carol had been to Ta Cenc since the film company had left, and it was strange to see it without any people: the waiting extras, the busy film crew, the small, bobbing figure of Varelle. And then she saw that she was not, after all, alone.

Sitting on one of the low walls, not very far from the frightening cliff edge, was a woman. She was very still, her hands in her lap. Beside her sat her little boy, round-eyed and restless, but the woman stared ahead of her, not talking to him. As she drew near, Carol recognised her as Rosaria, the dressmaker who had made her wedding dress.

'*Merhba*—how are you?' she said, sitting beside her.

Rosaria turned her face towards Carol. It was unsmiling, blank.

'Today,' she said, without any formal greeting, 'I will leave my husband.'

It was so unexpected, so stark, that Carol could not think what to say. She felt she must fill the silence, if only to lessen the bewilderment in the small boy's eyes.

'I am sorry,' she said.

'He has another woman, I think,' said Rosaria, a bitter note in her otherwise flat voice. 'Last night he came home at one o'clock, and he would not say where he had been. That is no good.'

'No,' said Carol, 'it is not good.'

'We have been married seven years,' the dressmaker went on. 'I have two other children. He should not do this to us.'

Carol listened while Rosaria poured out her story. It was a straightforward one, of marriage at eighteen, children, a husband who wanted to emigrate. Her parents had not liked him, Rosaria said, but she had stuck to him, even going to Canada with him and coming back when the success he had looked forward to did not come.

At the end of it, Rosaria's voice faltered, and the tears came into her eyes. She shaded them with her hand. Carol took her other hand.

'I wish there was something I could do,' she said.

Rosaria looked up. 'Perhaps there is,' she said. 'If you could speak to the Baron. He has been so good to us.' She held on to Carol's hand, clutching it as if it were a lifeline. 'When our little baby was ill, the Baron came himself to our house and took her to the hospital, and said, "You must see this baby, she is ill." I think that saved her life, then. And now—now, if he would speak to my husband, and tell him that he must not do this thing, he must not go with this woman, then I know that my husband would listen to him.'

Rosaria looked at Carol so pleadingly that she could do little else but promise to tell Nicolas all that the other had told her.

'But I cannot say what he will do.' she added.

'He will do what you ask him,' Rosaria said. 'I know that the Baron must love you. Your marriage is so new, so happy. He will surely, surely wish to please you.'

Carol could not meet her eyes. How could she tell Rosaria that the Baron did not love her, that he had no reason to do anything to please her?

Half-way back to the car, Carol looked round and saw Rosaria gazing after her, the child leaning against her knees.

She had no chance to carry out her promise until very late that evening. There was a dinner party at Xatahn, and Nicolas attended to the needs of his guests with extra care. Indeed, he made a point of seeing that no glass remained empty for longer than a moment, including his own. But although the conversation became louder and wittier, and the guests more and more relaxed, Nicolas remained the same alert and entertaining host.

Only Carol, who had to force herself to play the part of a poised and charming hostess, noticed the glitter of mockery in his eyes, and an impression of dangerous tension within the apparent good fellowship. She wondered if he was remembering their encounter in the cathedral, and knew he would not have missed the irony of the words she had used to describe their marriage.

When he had seen the last guests into their car, Nicolas did not go at once to his study, but came back into the big salon. There was irony in his own voice now.

'How pleasant,' he said, 'at the end of the day, to relax in the company of such a beautiful wife——' he refilled his glass, and raised it '—and one who makes so little demand upon my time or my attention.'

With a great effort, Carol answered him in a light, offhand manner. 'It seems to suit us both,' she said. And then, to change the subject, she told him about her meeting with Rosaria, and the request which the sad little dressmaker had made.

Nicolas listened in still silence, his expression unchanging.

'And how does she think I can help her?' he asked when Carol came to the end of her story. 'Does she think that I can work miracles? That I have the power to persuade a husband to love his own wife? It is as impossible a task, my dear Carol, as to make a wife love her husband if she does not feel so inclined. Do you think I have the power to do that?'

Carol shook her head. 'No one can do that,' she said in a low voice, and then made herself smile and say with an assumed brightness, 'That would be rather a miracle. It was stupid of me to bother you with such a problem, but she begged me so hard to speak to you.' The memory of Rosaria's pleading face came back to her, and spurred her on. 'She was so sure that you could help.'

'And what do you want me to do?' Nicolas said. 'I am not quite a feudal lord, my dear philanthropist. If he does not love her, it could be that it is her fault. Have you thought of that?'

'But the other woman!' Carol said.

Nicolas laughed, and there was a bitter ring to the sound. 'Perhaps there is no love in their marriage. Sometimes men are driven to other women . . .'

'Driven? By what? By their own natures!' Carol cried.

'How can I tell? A sharp tongue. Poor cooking. Poorer

loving. You collect proverbs—here is one for your collection: "A man who is hungry looks for food in a strange kitchen."'

'That's the most callous and heartless thing I've heard anyone say,' said Carol. 'Even you!' In her anger she did not see his eyes darken at the taunt.

He took a step towards her. 'Am I so callous?' he said softly. He was standing so close to Carol that she could see the deep lines about his mouth. 'That comes well from you, my dear.'

Carol looked away, but Nicolas reached out and took both her shoulders, turning her towards him.

'Look at me,' he said, and his voice was harsh. 'Be very careful how *you* accuse *me*.'

'Why?' said Carol. 'Why should I be careful? Is it because you are just another man like Rosaria's husband?' She was so angry now that she did not care what she said. 'Do you, too, look for food in a strange kitchen?'

She flung the words at him, and felt his hands tighten their grip on her shoulders, hurting her.

'Let me go!' she said, and tried to twist away from him, but Nicolas held her fast. The look on his face frightened her.

'Have you considered that I, too, might be hungry?' he said, and in the next instant his arms were round her, imprisoning her, and his mouth on hers.

Carol wanted to cry out, but she could hardly breathe. She wanted to escape, but she could not move. This was a different Nicolas from the man who had made love to her on their wedding night. There was no love in this hard embrace. Passion, yes; desire; and a hunger—the hunger of a man who feels compelled to satisfy that hunger, come what may.

And against her will, there was a force in Carol's body

which was hungry, too, which needed him, and cried out to him. But not like this, not with this Nicolas she did not know, this insistent stranger, not without love, without caring, not as if she were any woman, no matter who.

'All women are the same,' he had said to her once. And he cared for no one woman. The kiss which was threatening to overpower her could have been bruising any woman's mouth. The iron pressure of his arms could have been crushing the resistance from any woman.

If it had been herself that he wanted—wanted or loved— the strong emotions he was rousing in her would have been wonderful feelings, feelings that she could have given way to without reserve. But this was not a man who loved or wanted *her*. His only thought was mastery over her still-resisting body.

For resistance was her only hope. Not physical resistance; that was impossible with a man as strong as Nicolas. If it suited him, he would take her even if it was against her will, and this Carol thought she could not bear. Words were her best weapons—his own words to her, written so coldly in his cruel letter.

When the kiss, which was like a deep search into the core of her being, ended at last, Carol jerked her head back and away from Nicolas.

'Is this how you keep your promise?' she said, and heard her own voice as if it belonged to somebody else, breathless and quick, but as cutting as a small, sharp knife. It was his pride which she had to attack if she wanted to turn him away from her now.

She did not have to search her memory. She had torn up the letter, but she would never forget the words. 'Is this what you meant,' she flung at him, 'by promising to make no further claims upon me as your wife?'

Nicolas's arms dropped to his sides. He let her go. His

face was in darkness, and Carol could only imagine the expression in his eyes. At last he spoke, and his voice was as empty of passion as it had been tense before. If Carol had not been sure that he felt nothing for her, she would have thought that he spoke as someone who had been struck a blow. But the blow was to his pride, not to his feelings.

'I should need no reminding,' he said, so quietly that Carol could only just catch the words. 'You have made your dislike very plain. I regret that my ill-timed lovemaking should be so distasteful to you.'

'Lovemaking?' said Carol, and the bitterness in her voice was real and unmistakable. 'How can there be lovemaking between us, where there is no love?'

Still she could not see Nicolas's face. 'But of course,' he said levelly. 'That is something else I should not have forgotten. You will not have to remind me again.'

Carol covered her eyes with her hand. She did not want tears to come, not now. She heard his footsteps, and the door opening and shutting. Only then did she look up, and let her gaze rest blankly on the closed door.

CHAPTER TEN

AFTER a sleepless night of wondering how she could face Nicolas again after the events of that dreadful evening, it came as a relief to Carol to find that she would not have to.

'The Baron went away early this morning,' Anna told her as soon as she came downstairs. 'Charles went to look for the car, to clean it as usual, and it has gone. *Madame* should have told me.' She looked reproachfully at her mistress, and Carol tried to answer her without betraying her own ignorance of Nicolas's actions.

'It was a sudden decision,' she said, but Anna was not mollified.

'If I had known,' she said stiffly, 'I would not have baked all yesterday afternoon for the Baron's birthday.'

Carol was startled. She was Nicolas's wife, and she had not even known that it was his birthday. He had never told her; she had not asked. They were strangers living in the same house.

There was nothing now she could do to remedy that, but there must be something she could do to pacify Anna.

'I know!' she said. 'We shall have a tea party. Even if the Baron cannot be here, it will mark the occasion. And your baking will have been to good purpose.'

It was a blessing to have something into which she could throw all her energies so that she could shut Nicolas out of her mind. She had to make herself forget the way her body had wanted to respond to him, even though she knew there was nothing in his heart but physical desire.

If she were to survive at all, it must be by doing something—anything—to help her build a wall over the blankness in her life. In rapid succession she called for Jessy and told her to invite her sisters and any others who would like to come to the tea party, rang up Aunt Lucia and asked her to bring as many of the craftworkers as she could contact, reviewed Anna's baking, cajoled her into making another two batches of the feather-light little cakes she was famous for, and went down to persuade Cassar to let her have some of his loveliest pots of flowers and shrubs to decorate the two salons of the *palazzo*.

'We shall throw open the doors between,' she told Jessy, 'and there will be plenty of room for everyone who wants to come.'

Jessy was awestruck. 'You mean we shall be in the great rooms,' she said, 'to sit, like ladies, and drink tea?'

Carol smiled. 'Of course! And eat Anna's cakes. After tea we can walk in the garden. And if it is a success,' she went on, 'we'll do it again every week.'

The tea party was a success, and Carol did do it again. Thursday afternoons became gala days for more and more of the Xatahn tenants and craftworkers who came to the *palazzo*. Anna, after she had recovered from her surprise at the first experiment, entered wholeheartedly into Carol's new venture and took pride in producing cakes more delicious than any she had ever tasted.

'Nobody can resist your cooking,' she told Anna one Thursday morning, as she watched her decorating wafer-thin biscuits with curlicues of pink and white icing. 'That's what draws them.'

'Some will go anywhere if the food is free,' said Anna, but her broad smile showed Carol that she was pleased.

Three days after the first tea party, Nicolas had come

back, but his manner to Carol was so stiff, so reserved and formal, that she sometimes thought she would have been happier if he had stayed away. He made no reference to the scene he and she had played on the evening before his birthday. Words were not needed. His whole bearing made it only too obvious what he thought of the woman he had made his wife. Carol could read contempt in the turn of his head, indifference in the very silence between them.

She had little satisfaction in knowing that Nicolas thought her to be as unfeeling as he was himself. She feared that by hiding the real state of her heart from him so successfully, the time would come when pretence became reality and she, like Nicolas, cared for nobody and nothing. 'But isn't that what I want?' she asked herself. Wouldn't that be better than loving a man who did not love her?

Carol tried her hardest to shut Nicolas out of her thoughts, but this was made all the more difficult because so many of her Thursday afternoon guests loved nothing better than to talk about him.

'He is a good man. The best Baron of Xatahn there has ever been,' Jessy's married sister told her. 'He helps everyone. He does not keep his money for himself. He lend my husband much money for a new workshop. It is an investment for him, he told him, but we knew it was more good for us that for the Baron.'

'Yes, he is good,' said another. 'My brother and my cousin, they had a big quarrel about some boathouses. They could not speak of them without shouting. The Baron, he came, and he looked at the boathouses, and he asked to see all the papers, and he explained to my brother and my cousin, on and on, with much talking, talking, until at last they do not shout any more, and all is settled, and everyone is very happy.'

Carol listened with an aching heart. They were talking of an entirely different Nicolas from the cold stranger she knew.

It was on about the third or fourth Thursday that Rosaria came to Xatahn. She was no longer the sad distraught figure Carol had met on the cliffs at Ta Cenc.

'I decide to stay with my husband,' she told Carol in a low voice, while Jessy took her children outside to play in the garden. 'We have more work now,' she went on. 'The big hotel——' and she named the luxury hotel on the other side of Gozo '—they have a glass case with dresses and skirts in it. The guests can order, and then we make up, very very quickly, to fit them. Skirts for the evening, and for the beach, too.'

'I know,' said Carol. 'Like the floaty wraparound skirts you made for me?'

'Yes—you do not mind? It was the Baron's suggestion that we show some like that to the hotel.'

'The Baron?' Carol was astounded.

'Yes—did I not say? It was at the heats for the sulky races. The Baron was there, and my husband. They talked, and I do not know how it came to be spoken of, but it was a good plan.' Her face brightened. 'So now my husband does not want to go away, and he is more happy, with so much work. The Baron is a kind man,' she added. 'You must be very happy, to be married to such a husband.'

Carol hoped that her face betrayed nothing of her feelings as she murmured some reply. This thoughtfulness for Rosaria made Carol sad as well as pleased. If only Nicolas could have been as kind to her as he was to Rosaria, to every one of his tenants, to all the world, it seemed, except herself, how very different their life together could have been.

Nicolas spent most of every day away from Xatahn, and on some nights Carol did not hear him come back at all to the room next to the one where she slept alone. She tried not to give way to the thoughts which tormented her, but his words—'A hungry man looks for food in a strange kitchen'—went through her mind, over and over again.

She told herself that she did not care, that Nicolas could have as many mistresses as Solomon had wives, that it mattered nothing to her. But however hard she tried, she knew that this was an area where she could not deceive herself. She did mind. She minded passionately.

The nights were suffocating, and the days heavy, stealing away Carol's energy, and making her feel languid and headachy. Aunt Lucia was so full of her plans for her coming trip to Paris that she did not see how pale Carol was, and how little inclined to talk; she herself always had enough conversation for two.

Anna scolded Carol for her lack of appetite. Cassar minded his plants. And Ta Dentella came back from her holiday.

Carol was glad to see the old lace-maker again. She went to see her in her little house on the cliff at Ramla, and found her looking the same as ever. She was full of the time she had had in Malta.

'So many people!' she told Carol. 'In their hundreds. And the noise! Radios everywhere. I am glad to be back. My sister and her husband, they took me to see my nephew who is a fisherman, and my nieces who are married, all with babies—three more babies each since I saw them last.' She stopped, and took Carol's hand.

'And you?' she said, looking into her face. 'You are quite pale, I think. You do not look as well as a young wife should.'

'Oh, I'm very well,' said Carol, but it was not strictly true. She had known for some time that it was not simply the heat which was making her feel faint and queasy. Ta Dentella guessed how things were almost at once. She asked so many searching questions, and with such a warm concern, that Carol found herself admitting that she was indeed expecting Nicolas's child.

'Heaven bless you!' the old nurse exlaimed, her face alight with pleasure. She was so pleased, and so happy, that Carol tried to respond, and to pretend that she was as delighted as Ta Dentella assumed she must be.

But instead, she broke down, giving way at last to the accumulated unhappiness of weeks. It was a relief to lay her head on Ta Dentella's lap, and let her tears come unchecked.

'It is a time to be happy,' the old nurse said gently, 'not a time for crying. Do you think the Baron will not be pleased?' She stroked Carol's hair. 'When a man loves a woman, and she loves him, a baby is a wonderful gift from one to the other.'

Carol lifted her face, wet with tears. 'But you don't understand,' she said. 'The Baron does not love me. I don't think he can love anyone.'

Ta Dentella looked troubled, and rested her head on the high back of her chair. 'I have known him from such a long time,' she said, 'and I know one thing: he is proud, very proud. He is too proud, I think, to show that he loves. There is an old saying which begins "*Mara hobbha a turihiex*"— "Love a woman, but never let her know." It is stupid, but then a proud man is not always wise, even,' she sighed, 'such a clever man as the Baron of Xatahn.'

Carol was silent. She could not tell Ta Dentella why she was wrong about her beloved Nicolas, or that there was nothing between them now, on his side at least, but a cool, contemptuous unconcern.

'And you?' Ta Dentella's voice cut into her thoughts. 'Do you let him know? That you love him? And that you are carrying his child?'

On her way back to Xatahn, Carol considered the old woman's words. If only things were as Ta Dentella thought they were, how easy it would have been to tell him. But it was so long since she had told Nicolas anything, or spoken more than polite nothings to him, that Ta Dentella's advice served only to highlight the gulf of silence between them.

Carol could not imagine how she was to tell him that she was expecting a baby. She supposed she would have to, in time, but she could not bear that it should be the subject of one of their dry and distant dialogues. She could imagine his eyebrows lifting, as he said, 'Indeed?'

Nicolas had certainly noticed nothing so far, and indeed there was not much to notice as yet. In the mornings, when she left her breakfast almost untouched, he was already immersed in papers in his study, or had driven off to see to the installation of new machinery in the desalination plant. And in the evenings, when she again felt none too well, he was either out altogether, or came in so late that the dinners Anna had so skilfully cooked were spoiled.

'Why does the Baron not eat?' she complained to Carol. 'Yesterday I make for him his most favourite of all— marrow flower fritters—and he tastes them as if they were pieces of paper. I cook him ox-tongue casserole with wine, and he eats no more of it than would feed a lizard!'

'I don't know, Anna,' Carol said. 'Perhaps it is the heat. I don't feel very hungry myself.'

'Ha! That is a different matter,' said Anna darkly, and marched squarely off to her kitchens, leaving Carol to wonder if everyone knew about her condition except Nicolas, if he would be the last person in the *palazzo* to know, when he should have been the first.

Still she did not tell him. Instead, he told her that he had to go away again. 'I have to see someone in Rome. I may be gone two weeks, perhaps three. Will you miss me?' His eyes rested on her face, and his voice was casual.

Carol wondered fleetingly if the someone in Rome was male or female, and answered him with a coolness which matched his own. 'I shall try to survive,' she said, and gave him a social smile. They would always be strangers, she thought, and was relieved to be able to put off the ordeal of telling him her own news until his return.

'I'm sure you will,' he said. 'And Aunt Lucia will keep you amused.'

But Aunt Lucia was going away, too.

'August is a ridiculous time to go to Paris,' she said. 'No one there. But the Collections are on, and I must have something new to wear this autumn. And I usually scout round for a few knitworthy ideas for us. There's one place that does gorgeous stuff, can only be done with hand-spinning and hand-knitting, and we've plenty of both here.'

'Take some samples,' Carol suggested. 'Anna's niece has done a lovely one—so soft, it's like thistledown.'

'You're a genius,' Aunt Lucia told her. 'What will you do when I'm not here to bully you in the daytime? And no Nicolas to look after you in the evenings? My poor child, you'd better have my television set, or you'll die of ennui.'

In spite of Carol's protests, she brought it over on her way to the ferry, and watched Cassar install it in the big salon.

'It'll cheer you up, if it doesn't send you to sleep,' she said. 'And anyway, I can't bear to think of it being wasted.'

With Aunt Lucia and Nicolas both away, there was once more far too much time to think. Carol kept herself as busy as she could, taking over some of Aunt Lucia's liaison work in the mornings before it was too hot to drive about from one village to another.

She worked on her next fabric collection for Célie et Cie, but it was hard work; when she had more energy, she would find it easier, she hoped. For the present, she was trying out some new weaves for the weavers in the craft village, working them out on paper and a small hand loom.

There was still more time to fill than she liked, especially in the evenings. So she set herself to learn Maltese, and with the help of a dictionary tried out her new-found words at the Thursday tea parties, which led to much laughter and teasing from all sides. By now there was nothing left of the shyness and restraint of the early days, and when it was seen that the young Baroness did not mind how many mistakes she made, everyone was delighted.

One woman brought her a school grammar, and Rosaria an old exercise book.

'I know that you like the old sayings,' Rosaria said, 'and so I find this for you. I remember it from when I was at school, and the teacher made us copy them into our books.'

'Oh, but this is wonderful,' Carol said, turning the pages. 'And all written in both languages.'

'You can learn them for your homework,' said Rosaria, smiling, and Carol thought how different she was now from the sad-faced woman she had been.

It was just fate, Carol supposed, as she looked through Rosaria's old schoolbook later in the day, that all the proverbs were about love and marriage. Perhaps the teacher had known that the girls would like the more romantic sayings. There was a splendidly practical side to them, even so, which made her smile at first.

'The heart of a man,' she read, in Rosaria's schoolgirl handwriting, 'is like a cabbage, which he gives away leaf by leaf to everyone, but the heart he gives to his wife.' And if there is no heart? Carol thought. If there is nothing there to give?

She turned the page and came upon a saying which must have been a favourite, for Rosaria had decorated it with a curly border of daisy-like flowers. 'Look not at my face, look at my heart, if you want to know if I love you.'

But then Nicolas did not want to know if she loved him. The only pleasure it would give him would be one of power over her. She did not want him to know. So it was as well that he could not see beyond the mask, and into her heart.

The last saying had been added in different ink, but in the same hand.

'Marriage without lovemaking,' it stated, 'means sadness and sorrow.'

It was too apt. Quickly, Carol shut the exercise book and thrust it away from her. She picked up the letter from Aunt Lucia which had arrived that morning.

'Darling girl,' she read. 'The fashions are bizarre to a degree! You need to be either three metres tall or a creature from outer space. But some nice knitteds in some of the Houses, and Le Grand Tricot is mad about the thistledown sample, so I might do some business there.

'All the theatres are shut for the whole month, so I have only the cinema for amusement—which reminds me, your film has its première at Venice in September. Somebody I met at a party told me it will be ravishing.

Apparently the director is a Big Name, or he must have a good PR, as he's always popping up on TV chat shows here.

'Is that Nick of yours back yet? If so, give him my love and tell him to bring you to Paris in the autumn.
All love,
Lucia.'

Carol put down the letter with a sigh. She had not heard from Nicolas, nor did she expect to hear.

The house was quiet. Jessy had taken away her supper long ago, and she and Anna had retired to their own quarters. Although she felt tired and listless, Carol did not want to go to bed, not yet, to lie in the hot stillness of the night wondering where Nicolas might be, what he was doing, who he was with.

It was at times like this that she was grateful for Aunt Lucia's television set, though more often than not she fell asleep before the end of a programme, and then had to rouse herself to turn it off and go up to bed.

This evening Carol turned it on, and put her feet up on the *chaise-longue* to watch a documentary on birdlife in Africa. It must have had the usual sleep-inducing effect; she woke suddenly to the sound of a voice which seemed startlingly familiar. Opening her eyes, she saw Varelle's bearded face staring straight at her out of the screen.

For a moment Carol thought that Aunt Lucia's letter had given her a bad dream, but then the screen showed two men facing one another. Varelle was on the right, his pointed beard jutting out like a dagger towards the interviewer, a man she recognised as the compère of a weekly series on films, film gossip and film personalities.

'And what gave you the biggest headache when you were shooting your last picture?' he was saying now. 'Was it losing your leading lady before the end of the film?'

'That was not so bad, my friend. A leading lady is only a leading lady, *après tout*, because she is being directed by Varelle.'

Carol listened to his familiar voice. It was uncanny, hearing it here in the big shadowy salon. Only one subdued lamp shone, so that the lighted screen was like a window into a bright and different world.

'But to lose your leading actor as well—wasn't that a little worrying?'

Varelle vanished, and on the screen Tony appeared, leading a boarding party of sailors over the side of a ship. He was faded out to be replaced by the interviewer.

'And would I be right in saying that he and the leading lady had to be replaced at short notice? What is it like to direct inexperienced amateurs?'

Varelle's face filled the screen, frowning. 'A trial of my patience, but to such a man as Varelle, a challenge.'

'It has been said that you are almost as unscrupulous as Hitchcock in getting the results you want. Tell me, Director, is it really a fact that you once sent a spoof telegram to an actor who wasn't coming up to your very high and exacting standards?'

'But yes! I wanted him to be full of grief. "Show me some *douleur*," I said to him, "some great misery". And what does he do? He comes on to the set and looks as sad as if he is suffering from a little indigestion.'

'So you sent him a telegram?'

'Yes, yes, very urgent, to say that his wife was betraying him. And what happened? His grief was profound; his tears, they were so real—and his anger and bitterness! He should have won an Oscar for that scene alone!'

How very beastly of Varelle, Carol thought, remembering the boy and his rabbit.

'And did you have to use this kind of trick with any of the actors in *The Corsair Captain*?' the interviewer went on.

'Let me see. Yes, I did, right at the end of the shooting. It was the stand-in for the leading lady. An English girl, very *comme il faut*. She was supposed to be a reluctant bride—a forced marriage, you understand. She did her best, but she was like a puppet made of wood—a Pinocchio, all hands and feet and elbows.'

Damn him! thought Carol, remembering how he had begged her to save his wretched film, and she swung her legs to the ground, to switch him off.

'Leave it on,' said a voice from the darkness of the doorway—Nicolas's voice, low and tense, making her start. Nicolas! She felt as though her heart had turned over and was beating at twice its normal rate. How long he had been standing there she could not tell. She had heard nothing of his arrival, no car, no footsteps. He must have come in when she was asleep, and stayed in the shadows, not waking her.

'It was at the wedding scene, and at the rehearsal . . .' On the bright small screen Varelle was still talking, wagging his beard, looking pleased with himself. '. . . quite wooden. So when it came to shooting, with the cameras, I made a little subterfuge. With the help of one of my staff I arranged for a message to be slipped into her glove . . .'

Elaine, Carol thought, and a flash of memory, like a photograph, brought back a picture of Elaine saying, 'Stand still, while I help you on with the gloves.'

'. . . and when she took it off, before the ring was put on her finger, the paper would come with the glove . . .'

'Yes?' The interviewer was leaning forward, and, behind

Carol, Nicolas stood very still. She could not see his face, but the tension was a force which she could feel.

'A *billet doux*? And what did it say?'

Carol felt as if she were in the grip of a nightmare. She knew only too well what it had said. It had been no warning, only a trick, a hideous practical joke. 'Varelle's ruthless when it comes to getting what he wants,' Kate had said. He had wanted an effect, and he had succeeded. Did he know anything of the long-term effect it had had, on her life, and on Nicolas's?'

'Of course it was risky,' Varelle was saying. 'A surprise element like that would work for only one take, before questions could be asked. But as it turned out, one take was all I needed, as you will see.'

The picture changed to the wedding scene Carol remembered so vividly, from the slow procession to the altar to her frantic struggles to free herself from Nicolas's grasp while he forced the ring on to her wedding finger, until at the final words of the service she swayed and fell, a crumpled doll-like figure, to the ground at his feet.

'And on that note of high drama,' the interviewer said, 'we come to the end of our film celebrity interview with . . .' And this time Nicolas did switch it off.

CHAPTER ELEVEN

THERE was silence in the room. With the full realisation of what she had heard—what they had both heard—Carol felt stunned. Varelle! It was Varelle who had treated her as one of the pawns in his colossally super-egotistic game.

The silence grew in the darkened room, but it was a silence so taut, so tense, that it was frightening. After the first shock, Carol's feelings were in a turmoil. She felt a flood of relief that now, at last, Nicolas would have to believe her, but compunction, too; for how could a man like Nicolas, born with the knowledge that everything he did was right, face the fact that he had been wrong?

When she thought she could bear the silence no longer, Nicolas broke it, his voice as sudden as the first clap of thunder which comes before a storm.

'Not you! It was Varelle, not you. Not your doing!'

Carol heard her own voice, far away, as if it belonged to somebody else.

'No. No, I...'

'Then *why*? How could you let me go on thinking that you...' His voice was rough, angry—angrier than she had ever heard it.

'I tried to tell you. I *did* tell you,' she said, stumbling over her words, trying to remember. 'But nothing I said made any difference. You were so sure I was a liar, a scheming liar.' As she spoke, her voice was firmer, and she felt a surge of indignation coming to give force and point to her words. 'All you could think of was revenge. You were going to teach me a lesson, call my bluff. Don't you remember?'

She stood to face him, her hands clenched by her sides. Nicolas's face was still in shadow, and she could not see the expression in his eyes.

'I remember well,' he said, with a voice of steel. 'And *you*—you let me say such things and do what I did . . .' His voice was hard, and he took a step towards her. There was bitterness in every line of his face. 'Why? Couldn't you stand up for yourself? Why didn't you protest? Why did you let me go on believing that you—— In God's name, *why?*'

Carol felt as though Nicolas had hit her.

'What could I have done?' she cried. 'Thrown myself out of the tower you shut me up in? Stolen money to escape from the island? What *could* I have done against your colossal pride and—and—stubbornness, and your—your *blindness.*' She threw the words at him, words which now came all too easily, freed from long restraint. 'You wouldn't listen. You *refused* to hear my side. You never wanted to believe me, or even stopped to think why I should have tried to harm you, to have behaved like some female monster. And if you had listened, if you had *tried* to believe me, you would have made enquiries, you could have found Varelle . . .' She broke off. What was the use of saying 'I told you so' to Nicolas, of all people?

He stood so still that Carol wondered if he understood what she was saying. Never would she forget the smell of frangipani, nor the wall of noise made by the cicadas outside the open windows. But her words must have struck home, because when he spoke again it was in a tone so low that she could only just hear him.

'So there was no need for the marriage.'

'None,' said Carol, her anger spent.

'And there would have been no need . . .' His voice was still low, and he looked past her, through the long windows, as if he could not bear to meet her eyes.

'No need, after the wedding, for you to pretend that you cared anything about me. No need for such——' her voice faltered, but she went on '—such wretched, wretched misery for both of us ever since.' She felt the uncontrollable tears about to betray her, and knew she could bear no more. She neither knew nor cared, so she told herself fiercely, what his thoughts were; she would not wait to see what effect, if any, her words might have upon that stone statue of a man. She ran past him, out of the door, and up the stairs to her own room.

Sleep is a funny thing. It comes even at times when it is least expected: in times of grief or happiness, of excitement or despair. It came to Carol when she was exhausted by the storm of tears which had been gathering, and which had at last overcome her when she threw herself on the bed.

She was hardly aware of undressing herself, or creeping under the light sheet which was all that was needed on the hot and sultry nights. And when sleep came, it swallowed up her sorrow, her bitter words, and all the turmoil of her thoughts. She did not dream, but slipped into a blessed unconsciousness.

When Carol woke next morning, she felt as if all emotion had been washed out of her, leaving a blankness behind. It was almost a relief to feel nothing, to mind nothing, to answer Jessy's cheerful 'Good morning, *madame*' with something like serenity, and concentrate on drinking her coffee and eating the fruit Jessy had brought her.

Even when she heard Nicolas's firm step, and saw him

come out on to the balcony where she sat, she felt no alarm, only resignation, and even a stab of pity as he stood before her.

His eyes were tired, his face drawn, and the lines on it showed that he had had but little sleep, if any. He spoke with an effort, almost as if he had been rehearsing the words, and arranging them in his mind.

'It seems,' he said, 'that I have done you a monstrous injustice, an unforgivable and terrible wrong . . .'

Carol stared at him, her face blank. Was this really Nicolas speaking? She wondered what it could be costing him to admit that he had been wrong—more, that he had done her a wrong.

'A wrong which can never be fully undone. And . . .' he hesitated, but went on doggedly, as if performing a disagreeable penance, 'you were right when you accused me of pride. Only pride—headstrong pride—could have made me see things in such a false light. That, and . . .' he glanced at her, then looked away, 'some past history as well, which you may not know . . .'

'I do know,' said Carol. 'A little. I know that you didn't have much cause to think well of women.'

'I cared little about what happened to me, it was true,' Nicolas said in a flat voice. 'But to have forced you into an unwelcome marriage . . . It was unforgivable,' he repeated.

You don't ask me to forgive you, Carol thought, but aloud she said, 'It was my fault, too. I should not have given up trying to make you see . . .' And I loved you, said the small voice in her heart, shouting in the silence. I wanted to be married to you. But though her heart was crying out the truth, she knew that this was something she could not tell him—not yet.

Nicolas stared over her head. 'You do not have to play

the part of an understanding wife,' he said. 'I have been thinking of what can be done.'

Carol looked up. She had not thought ahead; she had not wanted to think. It was enough to hope that they might somehow begin again.

'One thing is clear,' he said, his face set. 'You must have your freedom.'

Carol found it hard to grasp what Nicolas was saying as he went on to outline the steps which could be taken for giving her a divorce, the need for a financial settlement—'Not that money can compensate for all you have suffered in this marriage; "wretched misery" were the words you used'—and the arrangements for her return to England as soon as she wished.

All this she heard in a daze, and then, in a moment, Nicolas was gone, and she was alone, with the words 'You must have your freedom—your freedom—your freedom' ringing in her ears like the blows of a hammer.

A red hibiscus nodded below her window. Carol knew that she must find somewhere outside the *palazzo* where she could escape from everybody. Anna would be coming for the daily menu, and Cassar would want her to see his new cuttings and discuss with her what plants should come in for the afternoon.

While she started the car, and put it into gear, and drove away—she had not decided where—her brain refused to do more than repeat Nicolas's words. 'Freedom, freedom—your freedom.' And his, she thought. Nicolas would be free, too, free of the whole tangled mess she had brought into his life.

Driving in the car was cooler than being outside in the still heat; the warm air blew through the windows as she rattled over the uneven roads, past houses where grass mats already hung over the doors to keep off the sun.

She made instinctively for Ramla, and then remembered that it would be full of people lying on the beach, and the hirers of umbrellas and sellers of fizzy drinks. She thought she caught a glimpse of Ta Dentella on the road ahead, walking back to her house from market, carrying a basket of vegetables. Carol knew that she would have to tell her what had happened, but not now—not now. Now that she knew for certain that everything was finished and over, she did not want to see anyone.

So she turned the car and drove back past the temple of Ggantija, through Nadur and out to the head of the little cove of San Blas. Few tourists found this little valley. The road did not go down to the sea. Only a double concrete track, deeply ridged to prevent a tractor or a donkey slipping, led down steeply to the black rocks and the small patch of sand which could just be called a beach.

Carol walked down this track to the sea. On her left the ground was baked hard, with deep cracks round dried and withered plants. On the right it fell away into tiny fields no bigger than roofless rooms, filled with fruit trees.

Carol could look down into them. Her eyes took in the small yellow apples, the lemons and the figs. Her mind worried a little about the problem of how very steep and hot she would find the climb on the way back. She heard the soft slide of the sea across the rocks below her, and felt a small wind on her cheek. But in her heart there was nothing, only a numbness, as if nothing mattered any more. Carol was surprised at the numbness. It was almost as if such major surgery brought its own anaesthetic with it.

At the bottom of the track a path of iron-hard grey earth ran to right and left, ten feet or so above the boulder-strewn beach. Under some sheltering trees Carol undressed and changed into her swimsuit. It still fitted, but for how long? she wondered, her mind still in neutral. Dimly she remembered the day she had bought it, so long ago, in London, so far away, in what seemed another life.

It was impossible to think that that could be her life again. There was nothing in that life she wanted to go back to now. Everything she wanted was here—friends, work, interest, even her vain hopes for love and happiness with Nicolas. They were all here in this island where the spell of Calypso had pulled her, and held her, reluctantly at first, and then a willing prisoner.

Feeling for safe footholds for her bare feet, Carol half slid, half climbed down the bank of prickly grass to the rocks at the edge of the sea, and waded into the warm and welcoming water.

As she swam out and away from the small deserted cove, she had a feeling, if not of happiness, at least of relief. Later on, when she went back, there were problems she would have to face, practical problems: where she would go, how she would live, when she would tell Nicolas about the child. But now, at that moment, there was only herself, and the blue water, and the horizon ahead.

Turning to look back, Carol was surprised to see how far she had come. The black boulders on the yellow sand, the grey parched hillside, the steep track, white like a scar, were small and clear and far away. Only one cloud made a dark blot on the painted blue sky.

To her annoyance there was a figure among the rocks, under the path where she had left her clothes. She had been so sure that here she could be on her own. The figure was waving, and shouting, though at that distance she could hear no more than a thin blur of noise, no words.

At the moment that she realised it was a man, and that

the man, unbelievably, was Nicolas, he made a swift racing dive from the rock and began to swim towards her. Carol knew that she had no hope of outdistancing Nicolas, but she did not mean to wait for him to catch up with her. So she swam on, ignoring the fact that her heart was beating uncomfortably fast, telling herself that whatever Nicolas had to say to her could no longer have any importance.

She would not even look back, and it came as a shock to hear his voice not twenty yards away.

'Come back!' he was shouting. 'What the devil are you doing so far out? Turn back.'

Carol went on swimming, fury growing in her at the command in his voice. It was only when he drew level with her that she turned her head to face him.

'Didn't you hear me?' he said, every line in his face showing anger, from the scowl on his brow to the grim set of his mouth.

'Do you never stop telling other people what to do?' Carol said, matching his wrath with fire of her own. 'Ever since you came into my life you've been giving me orders. Take part in the film. Come and be locked up in a tower. Marry me. Divorce me!' The fleeting thought went through her mind that for the first time Nicolas was on her level. It was strange to be quarrelling so violently with a face so close to hers. 'What can it matter to you whether I swim on or back?'

'Don't be a fool,' he said roughly. 'Of course it matters.'

'I shall come back when *I* choose,' said Carol, hearing the childishness of her words, and hating Nicolas for being the cause.

'Choose now, then,' he said, and reached out to grasp her shoulder.

Furiously, she hit out at him, only to have her hand caught in his.

'Don't struggle,' he said, 'you little fool,' but Carol fought with all her strength, lashing out with her other hand, trying to break free from his relentless hold.

'Do you want to drown?' she thought she heard him say, and felt the pressure of his hands on her shoulders, and gulped water as she went under.

For a brief but terrifying moment, Carol wondered if Nicolas did mean to drown her, to rid himself of her by a surer and more ruthless way than divorce. When she came to the surface again, she found that he had somehow manoeuvred her into the classic life-saving position, with his hands under her shoulders, and was swimming with powerful leg strokes back to the beach.

It was useless to fight Nicolas. All Carol could do was to let herself be pulled through the water. Overhead, the little cloud which had hung over the land was now much bigger, and darker, touching the edge of the sun.

When at last Nicolas slackened his grasp, Carol could feel sand under her feet.

'Is brute force,' she said, shaking with rage, 'the only way you know?'

They stood waist deep in the water, glowering at each other. The sky was now quite dark, and little silver spots appeared all round them in the sea.

'Out there,' Nicolas said, breathing hard, 'so far out, you might have been drowned. Storms come up so quickly. There are always accidents. You don't know what it can be like.'

'Then all your problems would have been solved,' Carol flung at him. 'No wife, no child, no dragging your precious name through the divorce courts!'

The silvery spots, which had been widely spaced, were now much closer together, and Carol saw, with a small shock of recognition, that they were drops of rain.

Nicolas made a move towards her, his face grim and set, and stopped, as with an effort.

'Don't say that,' he ordered her. 'Never say that.'

'Why not? You wanted me out of the way. The sea, or England—what difference can it make to you where I go, what I do? If you had let me stay out in the storm, no one would have blamed you. It would have been all my doing, not yours.'

The sea was almost black now. Out beyond the sheltering rocks, the wind whipped the water into hills. Inside the cove, where they both stood, the rain was falling in a drenching downpour, hammering at the sea, splashing their skin.

'But I don't want you to go to England,' Nicolas said, his voice harsh. 'I never did. Only that you . . . I thought it was what you wanted, all the time. To be free of me. To go back to your own country, your own friends.'

'As if you ever asked me what I wanted!' Carol said, with increasing anger. 'Never, in the whole time I've known you, have you even wondered what I wanted, or what I felt!'

'Is that what you thought of me?' Nicolas said, his voice low, tense. 'Carol, listen, you are wrong. Listen to me . . .'

'After the wedding,' Carol went on, her words spilling out as the rain fell faster—but not cold; it was warm, like tears—'when you made it so clear that I meant nothing to you, that I was only a cross you had to bear, even then, I found a kind of happiness here in Gozo. There was Aunt Lucia and her craftworkers. Anna and Cassar were kind, and Ta Dentella. And at Xatahn, I felt it was my home;

and then there was ...' She paused. 'And then, this morning, when you told me that I must go—*your* plan, *your* decision—it seemed there was nothing left, *nothing.*'

As the words poured from her, Carol saw that the tractor track was now a furious torrent of water cascading into the sea.

'Then stay. Stay at Xatahn,' Nicolas said roughly. 'I want you to stay.' His face was as dark as the sky above them.

'Why do you say that?' Carol cried out. 'Is it so that you can go on imposing your will on anyone and everyone? To feed your pride? Or so that you can humiliate me, and ignore me, again and again, and go off looking for what you call love in other women's arms?'

'Carol!' he shouted, and seized her by the shoulders. His eyes were so fierce, and so dark, that for an instant she thought he would strike her.

'Can't you see?' he cried. 'Don't you know the reason?'

'No!' Carol said. 'I can't think of a single reason that makes sense. Give me just one I can believe!'

'Because I love you!' he shouted into the rain, while the thunder rolled about the sky. 'Because I want you. Because, God help me, I cannot live without you.' His voice was lost in an exploding crack of thunder which tried to split the sky in two. As the blackness closed round her, it seemed to Carol that the end of the world had come.

When the dizzy blackness cleared, Carol found that she was in Nicolas's arms. His face was full of a concern which gave way to relief as she opened her eyes and looked up at him.

'Carol,' he said, and there was a break in his voice. 'My darling Calypso. You do have a habit of fainting in times of stress. Where would you be if I weren't here to catch you?'

He carried her in to the beach where the great boulders gleamed wet and black, and there was some shelter from the rain under a slope of rock. Here lay the clothes Nicolas had stripped off in such haste that only the shirt was not sodden, and this he wrapped round Carol.

She hardly needed its warmth. Pressed close to Nicolas, his arm round her shoulders, with the rain still falling round but not on them, Carol wished for no more comfortable place in the world.

'I don't understand anything at all,' she said. 'How did you know I was here?'

'Ta Dentella. I was searching for you. Nobody knew where you were. Someone, Rosaria I think, said you might have gone to the high cliffs at Ta Cenc; I was desperately afraid. There was no sign of you. Then I thought of Ta Dentella. She had seen you on the road to Nadur—she recognised the car.'

'Did she tell you . . .?'

'About the child? Yes, and so did you, when you were so angry that you didn't care what you said. But she told me something else—something I couldn't hope to be true at first. She told me that you loved me.' Nicolas looked down into Carol's face, and this time there was nothing guarded about his expression. 'My darling Calypso, why did you hide so much from me?'

'Why did you?' said Carol. 'I thought you hated me. Despised and hated me, at the beginning, and then, oh, the nothingness was worst of all.'

'And I thought you hated me,' said Nicolas. 'Loathed the sight of me. You would have had every right.' His arm tightened about her. 'You made it clear that you couldn't bear to be married to me. After I had left you that accursed letter, when I came back to Xatahn, your whole attitude showed me that you cared nothing for me.'

'That's what I was trying to show,' said Carol. 'It was all I could do. Have you forgotten what you implied in the letter, that you had tricked me into thinking you loved me? Before the wedding, right up to that night?'

'Our wedding night,' said Nicolas, and his fingers gripped her shoulder. 'That was no trick. There was no pretence there. Oh yes, I suppose I had been trying to make you fall in love with me, so that I could punish you for the wrong I thought you had done to me, to the family. And then, when I found that I wanted you so much, not from pride, not from revenge, but because—because you were you, because, I was furious to discover, I was in love with you, I had to fight it, hide it. How could I let you know? That's why I had to leave you. I knew I could never keep the truth from you the next day if I stayed.'

He stared out to sea, remembering. 'Even when I tried to convince myself that I hated you, I couldn't stop loving you. And I hated myself more, for being unable to conquer it.'

'So you wrote the letter,' said Carol, 'and went away.'

'I even tried to believe that you deserved it,' said Nicolas. 'God! How could I have been so wrong—so foolish and so wrong about everything?'

'Because you wouldn't let yourself believe you could be wrong,' Carol said, and laughed. It was wonderful to be able to laugh again. 'You had always been right, all your life. To be wrong, and on such a mammoth scale—it wasn't possible, not for the infallible Baron of Xatahn!'

His hand stroked her hair. 'Ta Dentella told me that I was a fool to hide my feelings. She said that I would lose you, you and our child, and that it would be nobody's fault but mine.'

'That's not fair,' Carol said. 'It was as much my doing, pretending not to care, thinking that I could stop loving you, trying to build up a wall of indifference against you. But I was so afraid of being hurt again.'

Nicolas groaned. 'And all the time, every time I saw you, I was longing to hold you, to break down your damnable self-possession, to kiss you until your coolness melted away. But you kept me at arm's length, until that evening when I lost control. You made it very plain then that you could not bear me even to touch you.'

'If only you knew,' Carol said, 'how much I wanted you to make love to me ... But not like that, not as an enemy ...'

'And then, when I found out about Varelle's inhuman trick last night, I didn't see how you could ever have felt anything but hatred and revulsion for me, after the way I had treated you. You had cause; God knows you had cause.'

'I tried,' said Carol. 'I tried to stop loving you, but I couldn't. All I could do was to hide it, not to let you see.'

'I was too blind to see,' Nicolas said.

'How could you see?' said Carol. 'You weren't able to look at my heart.' She paused at the question in his eyes. 'It's a saying. "Look not at my face, look at my heart, if you want to know if I love you."'

Nicolas smiled, and the harsh lines round his mouth vanished.

'Do you realise that nothing like you had ever happened to me before?' he said. 'Not even when I was twenty and thought I was in love for the first and only time. Didn't you feel it, too? That day at the carnival—I began to love you then.'

'I remember,' Carol said. 'I thought you liked me, at least. But there were so many stories.'

'Were there?' said Nicolas. 'Of me?'

'Tony described you as a kind of Bluebeard, and Elaine went out of her way to warn me . . .'

'You didn't believe them?' Nicolas said.

'Not then,' Carol agreed. 'They were too absurd. But later on, when you wouldn't listen to me, it was almost as if you did want some kind of revenge for what had been done to you, long ago.'

Nicolas gave a cry of protest. 'Don't remind me!' he said. 'Was I mad, Calypso? Could you stay married to such a madman?'

For answer, Carol smiled and looked up into his face, into the fierce question in his eyes. As his arms went round her, holding her fast, she could feel the power and the strength of his body against hers, and hear the beating of both their hearts.

'Madman and tyrant,' she had time to say, before his mouth came down on hers, stopping the need for words.

Outside the shelter of the rock the rain fell, gently, but neither of them noticed.

Later, much later, when the rain had ended, they walked up the steep double track together, the track which had been a raging waterfall and was now washed clean and glinting in the returning sun.

Down in the tiny walled fields on the left, the lemons gleamed bright among their dark and glossy leaves. And on the right, the earth which had been grey and parched was soft again, a reddish brown, bright with moisture. Fennel was growing there, the flowers yellow and alive. And, springing from the soft red-brown earth, small spears of grass were bright and sharp, like emerald stars.

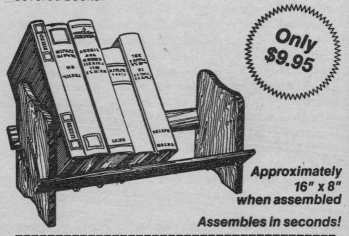

Harlequin Superromance

**Here are the longer, more involving stories you
have been waiting for...Superromance.**

Modern, believable novels of love, full of the complex
joys and heartaches of real people.

Intriguing conflicts based on today's constantly
changing life-styles.

Four new titles every month.
Available wherever paperbacks are sold.

Harlequin American Romance

Romances that go one step farther...
American Romance

Realistic stories involving people you can relate to and care about.

Compelling relationships between the mature men and women of today's world.

Romances that capture the core of genuine emotions between a man and a woman.

Join us each month for four new titles wherever paperback books are sold.
Enter the world of American Romance.

Amro-1

PAMELA BROWNING

... is fireworks on the green at the Fourth of July and prayers said around the Thanksgiving table. It is the dream of freedom realized in thousands of small towns across this great nation.

But mostly, the Heartland is its people. People who care about and help one another. People who cherish traditional values and give to their children the greatest gift, the gift of love.

American Romance presents HEARTLAND, an emotional trilogy about people whose memories, hopes and dreams are bound up in the acres they farm.

HEARTLAND... the story of America.

Don't miss these heartfelt stories: American Romance #237 SIMPLE GIFTS (March), #241 FLY AWAY (April), and #245 HARVEST HOME (May).

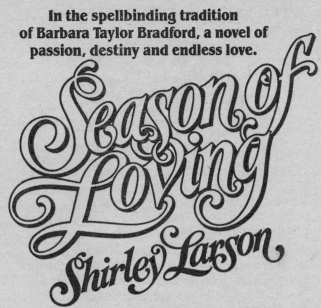
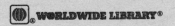